FOUNDER MEMBER

'Pure joy. An achingly funny, tongue-in-cheek thriller in which Boysie finishes up on a journey in a space capsule for which purpose you will discover when you read the book!'

Northern Despatch

'Not only action-packed but very, very funny.'

Coventry Evening Telegraph

'A brisk, flamboyant, fantasy à la Barbarella, with a definite "X" for sex.'

Birmingham Evening Mail

Also by John Gardner

John Gardner

Founder
Member

CORGI BOOKS
A DIVISION OF TRANSWORLD PUBLISHERS

FOUNDER MEMBER

A CORGI BOOK 552 08316 X

Originally published in Great Britain by
Frederick Muller Limited.

PRINTING HISTORY

Frederick Muller Edition published 1969
Corgi Edition 1969

This book is set in 11-12 pt. Baskerville

Corgi Books are published by Transworld
Publishers Ltd.,
Bashley Road, London, N.W.10.

Made and printed in Great Britain by
Cox & Wyman Ltd., London, Reading
and Fakenham.

'Ne'er will we e'er disremember,
E'en if axe our bodies do dismember,
Or our flesh is turned to ember,
This our gracious founder member.'

*Simpson's Anthology of Ancient
School Songs:* Translated from
the original Latin by Max Flasher

Permission to quote extracts from *Sea Fever* and *Cargoes*, both by John Masefield, is gratefully acknowledged to the Society of Authors as the literary representative of the estate of John Masefield.

CONTENTS

CHAPTER ONE

SOLOMON

Solomon of saloons
And philosophic diner-out.
MR. SLUDGE, 'THE MEDIUM': Robert Browning

BETWEEN four and five hundred of London's big double-decked buses pass by the Bank of England every day. To the casual observer it looks like they all gather in that area between five-thirty and six in the evening.

The Bank, the Royal Exchange and the Mansion House form a triangle which all but pinpoints the centre of the City of London – that grey sector which has been called the most important commercial square mile in the world: six hundred and forty acres within the confines of which the City of London Police wear red and white striped duty armlets, and money is the password.

On a normal weekday, the late afternoon traffic is vile; almost as bad as Paris; slightly better than the war fought daily at that time in New York. In the City, pavements become clogged with gentlemen dressed sober in black, identical in bowler hats, armed with meticulously furled umbrellas. They could be robot men leaving the factory for a test run; penny-in-the-slot men. (No. Five-bob-in-the-slot men: the City must take its percentage.) Tripping secretaries dodge between the money men and the air is heavy with speculation.

Leaving the City at this time of day demands skill, practice, determination and stamina. Getting into the City at the same time calls for similar qualities, plus the patience of a lion tamer, facets of character not possessed by the young man who was attempting such an upstream journey on this pleasant March evening in 1968.

To the uninformed, he merged into the surroundings like an egg in a grading factory. Pale faced from hours spent poring over figures, thin bodied, strong eyes set deep into his head giving the impression of twin stagnant rock pools, slightly effeminate hands with long fingers. Croupiers and trusted young executives of banking firms both have the same quick shrewd look. He could have been either.

His taxi had reached the top of Queen Victoria Street, and now both driver and passenger cursed, waiting to cross into Threadneedle Street.

The young man was visibly agitated even though he sat well back in the cab as if anxious not to be seen. The long fingers drummed on a slim briefcase, balanced flat on his knees like an invalid tray: an urgent impatience punctuated by constant peeks at his wrist watch.

He was already nearly an hour late and Sir Bruce did not like to be kept waiting. The young man, whose name was Bartholomew, became increasingly nervous about his reception. Sir Bruce's tongue had the burning quality of acid.

It was five minutes before the taxi rolled forward again, past the Bank into Threadneedle Street, drawing up opposite one of the many alleys which run, maze-like, at right angles from the rich thoroughfare. Bartholomew paid off the driver and hurried down the narrow side street.

It is in this part of the City the merchant bankers thrive and hatch their golden eggs. Innocuous doors lead to treasure caves; shop fronts, like original Phiz illustrations, hide undreamed-of fortunes. Bartholomew paused before an entrance decorated discreetly with brass plate, neatly engraved and bearing the names of a brace of banking companies. He glanced quickly to left and right, entered and began to mount the stairs.

Two floors above, six men waited, bored, around a mahogany table laid out with the precision of a statement of accounts: blotting pads, paper, minutes of the previous meeting, all the paraphernalia of a board of directors in session. One chair was empty.

The director of the board, seated at the table's head, remained aloof, his chair turned at an angle so that his face caught a long oblong of the sunlight's last rays.

He gave the impression, if viewed from the far end of the table, of one who is scrupulously clean in his personal habits, his movements and attitudes bearing those marks of authority which stem from the knowledge that money buys power. Age had not wearied him, neither had the years even begun to condemn. He could have been aged fifty or a late sixty, there were no guiding marks. A short man, his clothes were tailored with expensive care without being in any way florid or distinctively individualistic, while the silver mane topping an almost Roman head, could have been groomed from fine, carefully-matched silk.

Any journalist worth his salary could easily sketch in the man's background without putting a name to him. Town house, country house, in the Surrey Mida-mogul belt, possibly a villa abroad, certainly a Rolls-Royce, three-litre Rover, probably a Mini Cooper for luck. Profession: financier.

Though there was some kind of enigma about him, here was the nearest thing to a carbon copy of the popular picture of wealth: the stinking rich tycoon, the man who played Monopoly for real.

Three of the remaining five protagonists were miniatures of their chairman. Triplets: they thought alike, dressed alike and probably ate alike. In their own worlds they possibly spoke in terms of tens of millions and meant every five hundred thousand of it.

The fourth man was out of place. Small, nervous, like a grey rodent clad in worsted. One could only judge that his world was not that of his partners. It could be in the region of art, letters, science or even, at a pinch, religion. He had that vague fanatical look behind the bright darting eyes.

The last man, sitting to the chairman's right, was the least easy to categorize. He had the bearing of his more influential colleagues. The same smoothness and sense of authority. But something jarred. He was big, the shoulders standing out like twin promontories of rock, and a face which gave one the impression that the natural elements had bashed it hard and regularly. It was the face of a character actor long used to being cast as captain of an old clipper. A man who had served before the mast. This, coupled with a coldness about the eyes, made one feel that he was capable of carrying the ruthlessness of business into the bloody field of violence.

The chairman shifted his position from the dimming sunlight, allowing a half-inch of ash to fall on to the carpet from the smouldering cigar clamped between the first and second fingers of his right hand.

Looking briefly at his watch, he spoke. 'I presume he actually left on the flight we arranged.'

The hard man on his right paused in the act of kindling a cigarette. 'He did, Sir Bruce. And the aircraft left on time. I checked. Give him a chance. Not easy getting into the City at this time in the evening.' For all his brutal looks, the man's style and manner suggested a surface culture. Pleasant.

'I have to be in Woking by nine,' observed one of the affluent trio.

'Then if he's much later you'll have to phone and put her off won't you?' Sir Bruce's voice had a brusque unpleasant twang. Guttural. Something between Birming-ham and Berlin. 'We are all committed to this . . .'

The tap on the door cut short what was going to be a speech. Bartholomew had arrived, apologies fluttering like mating butterflies on his lips. Sir Bruce's patience had reached boiling point.

'Took long enough for you to get here,' he snapped.

'The aircraft was late. Then it was very hard to . . .' began Bartholomew.

'Save the excuses. Sit down.'

Agitated and fumbling, Bartholomew obeyed, taking the lone empty chair at the foot of the table.

All six men moved their chairs to get a better view, waiting with that expectancy usually identified with a dentist's waiting-room or the expectant fathers' lounge.

'Well?' Sir Bruce Gravestone was not noted for a gentle temper, but with Bartholomew he could hardly be less couth.

The young man swallowed, thyroid cartilage bobbing like a frenzied yo-yo. 'Their answer is . . . is . . . their an-swer is . . . no, sir.' Too loud and hurried for comfort.

The pause which followed was fractional yet it held the tension of ultimate catastrophe.

'Their answer is what?' The words came from Sir Bruce like individual pistol shots. He looked as though ready to spring at the man, animal passion ready to claw at his unfortunate underling's throat.

A further pause.

'Their answer is no, sir.' Bartholomew apologetic.

Sir Bruce sucked in a great lungful of air through his teeth. It made a strange whistling sound. 'Cretin. Moronic half-wit.' Sharp and clean as cheese wire. 'Why in God's name did I have to trust you?' He was on his feet, veins standing out on his face like rivers on a map. 'Bungling son of a bankrupt barmaid.'

'Please.' It was not a plea. Bartholomew seemed to

13

have got his second wind. 'I've got all the transcripts of my talks with the Minister. I've done my best. That's all I can do.' He was digging into his briefcase. 'I don't think anyone could have carried this one off. Not even Harold.'

'Harold who?' muttered one of the partnership as though lost.

Bartholomew took no notice. 'They sent this as well.' He lifted a long white envelope from the briefcase and passed it up the table to Sir Bruce. A crimson seal decorated the flap, round and splayed out like drying blood. 'I think the Minister will have explained the situation far more succinctly than I could ever hope . . .'

'More succinctly,' Sir Bruce mimicked, a podgy hand snatching at the envelope and ripping open the flap, sliding out its contents as a man whips out a worrying bill. Quickly he ran his eyes down the pair of typewritten flimsies he had removed.

'You stand over him with a gun?' He blasted at Bartholomew without taking his eyes off the papers.

'What?' Bartholomew, blank and urbane, his mouth open in a strange grin making his face momentarily assume the look of a death mask.

'This comrade is an ass. Positively nauseating about you.' He stared at Bartholomew, then turned to the remainder. 'Listen, gentlemen.' Reading in a clerical monotone. *'In declining your most generous and ingenious offer we must, however, pay tribute to, and congratulate you on your choice of emissary, Mr. Bartholomew.'* Spitting the name as a man fires phlegm from the back of his throat. *'He is a most persuasive talker and puts your case admirably and in vivid detail.'* Sir Bruce Gravestone leaned back, still scanning the document, blowing a long, straight stream of smoke along the table. Eventually he dropped the papers gently and looked slowly round the room as if memorizing each face. Silence except for the steady grumble of traffic floating in from the nearby teeming street.

Sir Bruce placed his elbows heavily on to the mahogany. 'It seems,' he said in a lower key, 'that our friends, while fully appreciating the project, feel they are already committed heavily with the *Lunar* experiment. They say there that it is impossible at this point to release a launch vehicle for such an enterprise.'

'There's also the question of their relationship with the British Government and that of not antagonizing the United States.' Bartholomew cut in, anxious to be of help.

'To hell with antagonizing the United States. Or United Dairies for that matter.' The baronet's words delivered with the force and effectiveness of a .41 Magnum bullet biting balsa wood.

'But we're so advanced. I have given so much.' The little animal man twisted his hands as though attempting to unscrew them.

'No tantrums, Schneider,' Sir Bruce calm again. The brief calm which could blow into a squall. 'We know of your brilliance. And we know this is very much your baby.' He paused as a chuckle went round the table. It was a chuckle of deference. The joke was not all that amusing. 'Just sit tight, professor. All will be well. Sit tight in your paternity space suit.' That was a better gag. The laughter more genuine.

'Bartholomew.' Sir Bruce looked straight down the table as the laughter subsided. 'I wonder if you would wait outside for a moment.'

Bartholomew looked startled, regained composure, nodded and left the room without speaking.

Sir Bruce smiled. The smile of a bank manager politely refusing an overdraft. 'Gentlemen. A word. May I first say that regarding this project the future may look murky to you. But remember I have splashed several million pounds from my own pocket into the venture. I refuse defeat. This is something that concerns not only ourselves as individuals but the cause for which we all strive.' He settled comfortably into his speech, enjoying the sound of his own voice. 'The idea for the project germinated, if that is the correct word, from the good Professor Schneider here.'

He indicated the grey worsted creature. There was a congratulatory murmur. Professor Schneider made self-effacing movements with his hands coupled with clucking noises from the back of the throat.

Sir Bruce continued. 'Professor Schneider and, of course, the other gentleman of whom we have talked a great deal.'

Schneider stopped the manual business and hen impressions, looking hurt at the mention of someone else sharing his personal glory.

Sir Bruce went on talking. 'You will remember that long before friend Bartholomew was dispatched to our friends we obtained written permission to use *Wizard* for research purposes, and that for an unspecified period.' He drew himself up to his full squatness. 'I am glad to tell you that all work there has now been completed and the date is set. Bartholomew was instructed to obtain the necessary launch vehicle together with official backing for the experiment.' Then, using that sepulchral tone normally reserved for senior members of the government during television broadcasts. 'To be honest, I saw that there might be problems. Those problems, as you have just heard, have materialized. But,' a finger stabbing the air as though dispatching a dangerous low-flying insect. 'But, you will notice that we have not been banned from using *Wizard* as an operational base.' The last words delivered like a card sharp with eight aces inside his cuff. He turned to indicate the man on his right.

'You are all aware that Solomon here is in charge of security.'

Solomon inclined his head.

'And it is to Solomon that we must now turn. He has come up with an idea of his own. All we really need is a launch vehicle . . .'

'A launch vehicle is all we need he says.' Schneider started repeating the miming tricks with his hands. 'A fortune it would take to build anything approaching the *Voskhod*.'

Sir Bruce looked at Solomon, passing the ball with his eyes.

'Professor Schneider,' said Solomon. 'I presume you wouldn't be averse to using a *Saturn V*?'

The Professor dropped his hands. 'The *Saturn V* is admirable. Already you have been told that.' He answered as though the whole thing was merely academic.

'Good,' Solomon replied as if clinching the deal.

'Before we go any further . . .' Sir Bruce interrupted, his hand on Solomon's sleeve, 'I think Bartholomew knows a little too much. He's a dedicated man but there are degrees of dedication. Some are more dedicated than others, like equality. Perhaps . . .?'

'I'll tell him to go.' Solomon rose. 'I won't keep you a moment, gentlemen.' He walked towards the door, remarkably light on his feet for such a large man. 'All will be taken care of,' he said, hand on the door knob. 'Then, Professor Schneider, I will explain how your work can become a reality.' He grinned pleasantly. A man who probably loved children and dogs.

The door closed.

'In spite of minor defects, Solomon is wise.' Sir Bruce crafty as a bent door-to-door salesman. 'I don't really think we're going to have a great deal of trouble providing a launch vehicle.'

Solomon was a wise man. Wise in the most deadly sense. Twisted, cunning, contriving, sly. A manipulator with an abnormally high IQ. His talents were many and rare, his contacts global.

Solomon was not his only name, he appeared in police files throughout the world under a multitude of anonymous guises. For the record nobody had yet succeeded in taking a photograph of him. In the markets of the Middle and Far East they spoke of him in whispers. The FBI would have liked a few words with him behind closed doors. So would Scotland Yard. European cops had itchy fingers for this large, ugly, smiling man with the deceptive powers of gentleness and persuasion.

In the anteroom, Solomon briefly told Bartholomew that he would not be needed until the morning.

Bartholomew looked relieved and departed smiling. Within a minute, Solomon was talking quietly into the telephone.

Outside, Bartholomew walked back down the alley and into Threadneedle Street, turning right and heading towards the Bank. He felt relatively carefree, having done his job as ably as he knew. Now, he looked forward to the pleasures of returning to his blonde house-mouse wife, Penelope, in Dulwich. He did not see the black Morris Oxford pull up a few yards behind him and disgorge a pair of neat young men.

By nine o'clock, Penny Bartholomew, the dinner spoiled, began to worry. At nine-thirteen she telephoned London Airport where they checked the flight and passenger list for her. Yes, Mr. Bartholomew was back in England.

At nine-thirty she called the office. No reply. She still hung on in hopes and it was not until nearly midnight that she rang the police. It did no particular good, for it was six months before they found Bartholomew's rotting corpse in a Buckinghamshire copse. And by that time it was all over.

CHAPTER TWO

STAR

And all I ask is a tall ship and a star to steer her by.
SEA FEVER: John Masefield

'FIRING command, thirty, mark.' The voice held that deep disenchanted quality which invariably finds its way into vocal service officialdom. It echoed through a dozen loudspeakers, and six times as many headsets inside the launch Control Centre.

'Roger. Periscope has retracted.' A lighter shade, crisp, matter of fact, difficult to believe that it came from a human on the brink of space.

'*T* minus two minutes forty-five seconds.' The launch Supervisor, earnest, crew-cut and cool, spoke flatly into his microphone. The big Neon Digital counter relentlessly subtracted the seconds towards zero; conditioned eyes were steady on television monitors; needles quivered in readiness, or already flickered their nervous curves on slowly moving graphs within the telemetering systems; a couple of hundred switches began automatic reaction. The additional one hundred and ten combinations of control, communication, display consoles, power panels, patchboards and computers which make up ACE s/c (Acceptance Checkout Equipment – Spacecraft) were giving green lights.

Way out in the cold grey morning, which betokened a later heat, across the uninspiring one hundred and twenty acres which makes up Launch Complex 37 at the northern end of Cape Kennedy, the beast, white tipped, pointed critically towards the sky: a *Saturn IB* rocket, separated now from its gargantuan gantry, gripped by the hold-down clamps against the moment it would be unleashed, a mist of spray rising around its first stage as tons of water flooded on to the launch pad cooling the vicious heat.

Commander Rupert Birdlip, one of the many Intelligence Officers assigned to the National Aeronautics and Space Administration turned to Boysie Oakes and whispered. 'From here on in, the countdown is computerized, but you'll hear them call the last ten seconds.'

Boysie did not speak. To all intents he was caught up in the tension of the moment, icy eyes narrowed, fixed on the tall finger of hardware out on the launch pad. Like a child, it was the moment to which he had looked forward for days, yet, now it was here, his mind kept leaping back to the night before last. Leaping like a rampant antelope. Jumping back to his old playmate Chicory Triplehouse. There was a warm feeling around his loins as he gazed at the rocket, pondering on his reunion with the concubinatious Miss Triplehouse.

Standing close, Birdlip sneaked glances at Boysie. It was four years since he had seen the tall, tanned Englishman, and Birdlip thought he detected some changes.

In 1964 Rupert Birdlip had been stationed in San Diego, and his involvement with Boysie, at that time, led to a frantic experience almost ending in court martial.*

In those days Boysie seemed more anxious in manner. Now, there was a relaxed toughness about the man, a mature self-confidence which Birdlip could not associate with the friendly buffoon who had caused such havoc out in sunny San Diego Bay. Perhaps, he thought, it stemmed from the change in Boysie's circumstances, the switch from those rigorous hazards of official undercover in-

* See *Understrike.*

20

trigue to the more gentle conditions of a private security organization.

There had been changes in Brian Ian (Boysie) Oakes' nature. Superficial, but real enough. In spite of having an enviable physique and rugged good looks, Boysie had capitulated to the doctrine of confirmed cowardice early in life. Added to this he was a clown, it was part of his basic nature.

His ambitions were not far removed from those of most men – a horn of plenty, his own castle (a penthouse would do) and an inexhaustible supply of young women yearning to be cherished by him alone. To give credit, Boysie had, at one time or another, managed to achieve most of those dreams. Albeit at the cost of self-knowledge and a closetful of screaming neurotic skeletons.

But, in some senses, Birdlip was right. After a number of years with British Special Security, served more by accident than choice, under Colonel James George Mostyn, the most sadistic boss for which anyone could wish, Boysie had suddenly found himself free and in from the chilly confines of spyland.

If Boysie dreamed of retirement to the traditional cottage with roses round the door he was out of luck. Mostyn was a hard man to shake off. Mostyn was also out of a job. Within a short time of finding his new democracy, Boysie was catapulted into a new kind of business. The superficial special swinging detective type security agency which Mostyn had dreamed up. With headquarters in Dolphin Square, lots of contacts from the old days, and a staff recruited from former members of Special Security, the firm, GRIMOBO ENTERPRISES, was headed by Mostyn, Boysie and their old unofficial colleague Charlie Griffin.*

Like most cowards, Boysie had the ability to slip on the cloak of bravery after the event, and, while there were

* See *Madrigal*.

the occasional nightmares, his memory played the ultimate trick of deception. Now Boysie looked back on his time with Special Security as a period of great stimulation, seeing himself as a hero in the mould of the great fictional dare-devils.

Paradoxically, Boysie had the measure of himself in other ways. After rattling round the world, playing at being the poor man's Don Juan, he saw that a part-sophisticated oaf in his mid-forties cut a somewhat ludicrous figure. Trying to display virility, playing the teenage field and whooping it up in fast crimson sports cars was not really his style. But, like so many men, the various disguises he had been forced to assume led Boysie into whole stretches of time when truth and reality stumbled, fuzzed-up and dodged the issue. It was during those periods that he passed himself off, quite seriously as a ruthless personality, desperate, well-connected, equally well-educated, and with a family background which would make even Tony Snowdon look like a fake.

Yet, if honest, Boysie would admit to the old churning in his stomach pit, a natural warning of disaster ahead, when, two weeks previously, Mostyn announced his intention of leaving for New York.

The three directors of GRIMOBO had just concluded their usual Monday morning meeting when Mostyn dropped his grenade.

'That's nice,' said Griffin, mistrust splitting the vocal seams. 'We got a job there or somethin'?'

'Not yet.' Mostyn, bland as ever. 'I've a few business arrangements to make.'

'Private business then?' Boysie trying to sound unconcerned.

'No.' Mostyn secretive.

'Then who's paying?' Boysie using a rapier as a bludgeon.

'The company of course.'

'Ah,' grinned Griffin. 'Then if it's company business we got to 'ear more. 'Ent we, Boysie boy?'

'I should bloody well think we have got to 'ear ... hear, more. Swanning off on company business to New York without even a by your leave ...'

'... from your fellow directors,' Griffin finished.

Mostyn contorted his face into the trickiest of smiles. 'Hold hard, brethren. Don't you trust me?'

'No,' said Boysie with feeling.

'Not where the company's money's concerned,' retorted Griffin. 'Sooner trust the government than you, and that's sayin' somethink.'

'We're not invited?' Boysie joined in on the make.

'I see.' Mostyn paused as if trying to think up a suitable excuse. 'Naturally, Oaksie, I was going to consult both of you. My feelings are that we should back the old economy and become dollar earners.'

'Dollar earners,' repeated Boysie.

'Precisely. I'm travelling to New York, that great city wherein pounds the very heartbeat of democratic freedom, in order to set up an American branch of GRIMOBO ENTERPRISES. What could be better than that?'

'All three of us going to New York to set up an American branch of GRIMOBO ENTERPRISES,' parried Boysie.

'Yerse,' said Griffin.

'Yes, my dear blue-based boobs, but who'd mind the store here?' Smooth and sticky little Mostyn.

'Everythink's 'unkey dorey 'ere. Martin can look after this end for a couple of weeks. No problem.' Griffin was sold on the idea of a jaunt to the big naked city.

'I wouldn't leave cheery benighted Aston to look after the tea money,' reacted Mostyn.

They argued. For half an hour. Mostyn even resorted to the gin bottle. But Boysie and Griffin were adamant. If the firm's money was being used to set up an office in

23

New York, then the whole trio had to go. All for one and one for all, or something. 'Those Three Muscatels and that,' said Griffin.

Mostyn eventually cut his losses and gave in. 'All right. It's a bloody waste of money, three of us going instead of one, but if you won't trust me, then you . . .'

'Won't,' chorused the other two.

'Then there's nothing more to say.'

'Ah.' Boysie's mind suddenly elsewhere. 'How far is Cape Kennedy from New York?'

'Oh my hallowed aunt.' Mostyn lifted his piggy eyes heavenwards. 'You and your bloody space ships.'

The whole staff knew of Boysie's latest craze. His flat was littered with plastic kits of satellites, space capsules and rockets, while the bookshelves bulged with science fiction.

Mostyn sighed again. 'Cape Kennedy, Boysie, is a considerable distance from New York. Over two hours flying time. And I don't think they're going to let you, of all people, go and play with their rockets. We had enough trouble with you on Guy Fawkes' night. Remember?'

Boysie remembered. Vividly. The rocket cost him five guineas at Hamley's and the fire brigade was not impressed. 'How was I to know the trajectory would go all wrong?' Boysie sullen.

'It should not have gone as wrong as it did. Only an idiot could have allowed it to be lethally propelled through a half-open window. A half-open lavatory window where a dowager duchess happened to be recovering from a severe bout of dysentery.'

'Dysentery my eye.' Griffin came to Boysie's defence. 'Touch of the shits she 'ad. Dysentery, that's only what the bloody upper class calls the screamers.'

'And you didn't help matters.' Mostyn fixed his eye on Griffin. 'Making witticisms to the insurance people. Saying must have been something she ate.'

'Well, it only burned 'er drawers. She got out before the thing exploded . . .'

'Badly damaging one wall . . .'

'. . . and smashing a brand-new lime green . . .'

'Tremble chair,' interpolated Griffin once more.

'Lavatory pan,' corrected Mostyn.

Boysie choked at the memory. 'And sent a roll of matching Double Delsey shooting out of the window like a smouldering gas bomb.'

'It was not funny.' Mostyn slapped the table, trying to bring the conversation to a halt and convince himself of the lack of humour afforded by the situation. 'Right, let's get back to New York. What we want there is a girl with enough intelligence to sort out the sheep from the goats, keep a communications' centre open . . .'

'You don't think I could wangle a trip to Cape Kennedy, then?' Boysie refused to give up.

'Oakes.' Mostyn's jaw closing like a man trap. 'This is a conference which might have far-reaching effects upon our financial status, but for the record, I do not think you have an iced lolly's chance in Equatorial Africa of getting a look round Cape Kennedy.'

Boysie grinned. Mostyn had not taken into account the fact that, since their terrifying visit to San Diego, four years before, Boysie had kept in touch with Rupert Birdlip. And Rupert Birdlip was now deep in the heart of the National Aeronautics and Space Administration.

It took a couple of transatlantic calls, on the firm's account, for Boysie to get the scheme going. At first, Birdlip was a shade cool. Boysie could not be classed as service personnel any more, which made things impracticable. But finally he agreed to bend the rules and pass off his guest as a visiting British space scientist. Dates, times and flights were co-ordinated. Boysie licked lips in anticipation, for his social call on Cape Kennedy coincided with a launching in the Apollo Series.

Leaving London Airport, or any airport, was a testing time for Boysie. On this occasion the unpleasant pangs he invariably felt when flying were made considerably worse when, as they entered the first class cabin, Boysie glanced towards the flight deck and noted that the entire crew of their Super VC 10 appeared to be studying an instruction manual, brows creased with the look of incomprehension. Boysie recalled that other time, when, seated ready for take off the stewardess announced, 'Captain Griffin and his crew welcome you aboard. . . .' More superstitious in those days, Boysie had needed gigantic reserves of self-control to remain strapped in with a picture of his Mr. Charles Griffin, murder bent at the controls.

On this trip, however, even Boysie's natural aversion to flying was eased by the thought that he had put something over on Mostyn. Throughout the flight, he smirked quietly to himself, or slyly at his senior director. Boysie would cheerfully have walked a couple of hundred miles, with dried peas in his shoes, wearing a monk's cowl, merely to score a gleeful point off snide James George Mostyn.

Arriving at some large city after a long flight invariably gives one a sense of superiority. People on the ground have been sweating out their menial tasks through the day, while you have been close to the gods, shrieking it along the jet stream. Boysie edged his mind into this attitude as, in the wake of Mostyn and Griffin, he passed through the endless formalities of arrival. Their BOAC VC10 had touched down at about four-thirty in the afternoon – just in time to hit the inevitable rush hour traffic of Manhattan.

'Think we should try for the helicopter service into the city?' asked Mostyn when they were through passports and customs.

'Sadist,' breathed Boysie.

'Git some right effective shots that way.' Griffin was all tourist, movie camera at the ready.

Aloft again, Boysie's face flecked with a colour that would have gone well with Picasso's *Young Woman Drawing,* they chopped in over Queen's and the East River towards the glittering clusters of concrete and glass stalagmites sprouting from the island of Manhattan.

It was a crisp clear evening, and Boysie realized the truth of the old saying that when you are in New York it is the city you most want to get away from, but, once away, it becomes the city to which you must return. From helicopter view the parallel lines of main streets looked like symmetrical ant runs, while a glimpse of the wide oblong of Central Park brought from the normally un-movable Mostyn a sincere, 'Quite a city.'

Boysie's stomach cartwheeled as the needle point of the Empire State seemed to tilt ominously, then it steadied and they were smoothly descending onto the white landing circle high above Park Avenue on top of the Pan-Am Building.

It had taken them only a matter of minutes to cross from Kennedy to the centre of Manhattan. It was a good half-hour before the trio made it up the few hundred yards of Park Avenue to the Waldorf Astoria Hotel. Crammed, the Fords, Chryslers and Cadillacs moved bumper to bumper up what is now one of the most commercial streets in the world.

Among the great glass-walled buildings which have sprung up along this once lush residential area, the Waldorf Astoria Hotel remains strangely anachronistic, even with its twin tower skyscrapers.

Boysie paused under the hotel awning to ogle the ITT Building and Union Dime Savings Bank across the asphalt prairie of divided thoroughfare. The noise was like nowhere else – traffic, doormen's whistles, loud, brash.

Not really so much of a noise as some crazy symphony which slid like a pile of bacteria into your blood stream and shot wads of static into the nerve centre of your body. The song of New York; the tingling pitch of the city. And all mixed up in it were the tantalizing scraps of half-heard conversation.

'So she says to me, 'Hot Dog, mister?' And I come back with 'I already got one, sister.' How about that? You get it? I already...'

'Joe, I swear to you I am never. And I mean it, Joe. Never, never going through that ordeal again. Never...'

'Ah, kiddy, that broad. It was like laying a hard boiled egg...'

'If you don't ask you never find out, so I said...'

'Then I found I hadn't put them on after all. Was I ...'

'And he died. Just died there in the office.'

'Terrible.'

'What do you mean, terrible? I'd been after that guy's job for seven years...'

'She'll know about it. Tonight she'll know about it...'

Boysie followed a bewildered Griffin and ever-suave Mostyn through the doors, up the marble staircase and into the gilded lobby where, many say, people actually live, sleep and abide.

Mostyn, being Mostyn, had acquired a suite, with main lounge and three bedrooms on the twentieth floor. A thick expensive envelope, the kind you get from wealthy charities, addressed *Colonel F. G. Mostyn,* lay waiting on the bureau. After they had washed, called room service for drinks, examined the decor (lapsed Regency), fiddled with their TV sets, Mostyn tore open the envelope and called the meeting to order.

'It seems,' he began pompously after scrutinizing the contents, 'That the agency has five possible girls.

We start interviewing tomorrow aft ...' A knock at the door.

After years of uneasy living, Griffin's hand lifted quickly to the inside of his jacket. Boysie loped lazily over to the door and opened up, revealing a diminutive messenger boy, cap in one hand, envelope in the other.

'A Mr. B. Oakes?' queried the messenger.

'In the flesh,' smiled Boysie.

'Sign please.'

Boysie signed and took the envelope. The door had hardly closed before he began to open the flap. It appeared to be twice as bulky as Mostyn's.

'CIA probably want you to sort out a couple of problems for them.' Mostyn's sarcasm was fringed with irritation.

Boysie scanned the typewritten notepaper. 'Hardly,' he said, unmoved. 'Terribly sorry and all that, but 'fraid I won't be able to help choose the right girl tomorrow. Going to have a look round Cape Kennedy. My own money of course.'

Mostyn visibly called upon his personal guardian angel to give him strength. 'You are going up to Cape Kennedy tomorrow?' He spaced the words, letting them drop like icicles.

'Fly up to Melbourne, Florida – oh, I will be able to help. Don't leave until five-forty-five in the evening. Back the following afternoon. Old Rupert Birdlip's fixed it. Remember old Birdlip? San Diego?'

'I remember Birdlip.' Mostyn's lip twisted, the villain in a Victorian melodrama.

'Good song title that.' Griffin perky, waiting for the confrontation to explode into a shooting war. 'I remember Birdlip and my heart still sings.' He warbled in a stucco off-key.

'Shut up.' Mostyn in black fury. 'As we cannot start interviewing the girls until three-thirty I do not see Boysie being much help. Which means,' He chewed the words like mincemeat, 'that you, Boysie bloody Oakes, are a fellow traveller.'

'So sue me.' Boysie turned away quietly singing *Lullaby of Birdland,* substituting Birdlip where necessary.

'I'll do better than sue you, Boysie my old mate, I'll charge your share of this excursion to your salary.'

'Okay.' Boysie shrugged. He had expected it anyway and the victory was choice, even though Mostyn did not speak a single word to him until after his return from Cape Kennedy.

Boysie stuck it for half an hour while Mostyn pontificated to Griffin about the New York office and its prospects. Their senior partner was becoming horribly repetitive. At last Boysie got up and casually sauntered towards the door. Nobody tried to stop him.

In the elevator, alone but for the operator, Boysie made a blatant study of his reflection in the long mirror. Age, he thought, was a strange thing. In childhood one imagined the years between forty and fifty to be an age of great wisdom. Or a time when you were washed up, on the beach with sand nagging at the wrinkles, senility coming on target fast.

Yet, when you reached, and passed, your two score years you did not feel much different. The same old desires and the same treacherous mistakes. He looked at himself, carefully tailored in his second best grey. Mauve shirt and black tie discreetly spotted with matching mauve dots. The line was good. In the mauve if not quite in the pink. In spite of the overdoses life had offered, his face had taken it pretty well, the eyes still clear, the hair line untouched by time's erosion.

'Main lobby.' The elevator boy broke up Boysie's narcissistic affair with the mirror.

'Come on, lad,' he said to himself with a sidelong glance at the reflection, 'Be your age.'

The action was centred around the bar in the main lobby. Boysie chose a table, ordered a cognac, and sat back to take in the dizzy square scene.

During the early evening, the lobby of the Waldorf Astoria has the faint flavour of a theatre foyer on some bizarre first night. You have the feeling it has all happened so many times before. Really you don't want to know any more. Fifty per cent of the folk who trip and totter through that hallowed area at the cocktail hour look as though they ought to be known. The remainder desperately want to be known, or at least needed and cared for. A grazing pen. Fodder for the analysts' leather couches.

It was, thought Boysie, like a velvet and scented railway station where, if you were lucky, one evening could reward you with the glimpse of some face fitting an international name. The hand of dead luxury fingered scarlet drapes. All was gilt, gingerbread; cosmetics, to set the clock back; perfume, to put it on; faces in search of reassurance: bodies probing desperately for relief. Old schoolfriends (Class of '19) were reunited; spiteful little dinner parties gathered momentum, grew, became swollen with gossip as they headed for the restaurants where they would finally explode in a fallout of smoked salmon and rare Adam rib. Middle-aged men felt life stirring for the first time as they looked into the deadly eyes of vibrant teenage girls who may, or may not, have been their daughters.

People, thought Boysie Oakes, stank. On every strata they reeked. He dropped his head, looked at the cognac, decided that he niffed more than most and downed the biting amber liquid in one. Lifting his head again, Boysie's eyes zoomed in like a movie camera, focusing clear on a white dress overlaid with shimmering organza nylon, the dress itself hanging in the simple line of an underskirt. A seven pound lead weight seemed to attach itself to Boysie's jaw. His eyes brightened and morals began their take-off run.

The dress covered a body he knew. Golden, lithe, leggy. You name it, this one had it, right up to the tawny hair piled neatly above the familiar face.

The girl had not seen him. Boysie edged from his chair and moved round the slum areas of the lobby crowd. She was conspicuous and kept tapping her foot, indicating that she waited for some tardy male.

Now, Boysie was behind her, advancing quietly on that back he knew so well. He stopped a pace away, then moved in close, speaking softly out of the corner of his mouth. 'Okay sister, just standing there you're infringing some by-law so let's go.'

'Get lost buster I . . .' She turned and let out a shriek of joy, stopping the world for a good ten seconds. 'Boy-SIE.'

'The Triplehouse girl from Joplin, Missouri.'

Chicory Triplehouse held him at arms' length, studying the picture. 'You don't change. Not one bit. Hey, what're you doing here anyway? No, on second thoughts don't tell me, let's get the hell out of here. I got a date and he's already four minutes late.'

'In my book that makes sacrilege.'

'Sacrilege in a pornographic book?' Chicory raised her eyebrows in a great arch, linked arms with Boysie and hustled him towards the doors.

Boysie and Chicory had first met during the same disastrous summer that Birdlip came into contact with Oakes and Mostyn. Now, standing next to Birdlip, watching the monitors, listening to the staccato procedure, Boysie could not get the luscious Triplehouse, and what followed on leaving the Waldorf Astoria, from his mind.

'Main buss twenty-four volts, twenty-six amps . . .'

They had taken a cab straight to her place, still the same apartment high over Fifth Avenue, with the big mirrors and golden wallpaper that matched her skin.

'*Ten . . . Nine . . . Eight . . . Seven . . . Six . . . Five . . . Four . . . Three . . . Two . . . Zero . . . Ignition . . . Lift off.*'

The cluster of eight H-1 Rocketdyne engines started their incredible roar of power, beginning to burn up the Rp-1 fuel and Lox. Soon the first stage thrust would develop to 1,600,000 pounds. An inferno of crimson; a mushroom of smoke. Dante would have been at home down there below the rocket. Slowly the slim projectile rose.

'*Roger, lift off and the clock is started. . . . Apollo Two fuel is going, one decimal two G; cabin at fourteen psi; oxygen is go . . . Apollo Two still go . . . Fuel is still go; One decimal eight G, eight psi cabin and the oxygen is still go . . . Cabin pressure holding at five decimal five. . . .*'

Boysie knew well enough what Chicory meant by the pressure of her fingers on his arm. Their personal ignition and lift off was, had been since that summer of '64, as spectacular, in its own way, as the *Saturn B* lifting out on Launch Complex 37.

Their kiss, her back firm against the door was like a deep dive into clear water.

'It's been a long time, Boysie,' she said as they broke surface. It was standard stuff but sounded different from her.

'Remember the first?' He undid his tie.

Chicory smiled, unzipping her dress.

'*Fuel is go. Two decimal five G. Cabin five decimal five, Oxygen is go. Main buss is twenty-four. Isolator battery is twenty-nine . . .*'

'Aren't these grippernickers a gas, Boysie?'

On her they looked splendid, firm, small, holding tight,

white as a boiling sea fringed with a tiny stimulant of lace. Chicory's hand went up to her brassiere and it dropped to the floor as Boysie stepped out of his trousers. Her breasts still had that magnetic curve calling out for a hand to caress, a pair of lips to brush the nipples.

'Gee, I think it's great men are wearing sexier under-clothes now.' She needed to talk. With Boysie words were not necessary.

Boysie stood naked but for the tiny bulging blue nylon briefs.

Chicory's hands went to her pants, thumbs hooking into the waist, peeling them off like cellophane from a cigarette packet. Boysie, eyes never leaving her, stepped from his briefs and moved close.

'All systems go. Projected out Okay.'

'Fuel is go. Four G. Five decimal five cabin. Oxygen. All systems are go ... It's a lot smoother now. A lot smoother now. A lot smoother.'

'I see you've started shaving.' Boysie's hand hard, high between her thighs.

'Like it?' A kiss stopping the answer.

'Smooth.'

'You must recommend a good foam.'

'Always use the best.' Another kiss.

Her hand was on him, pulling. On the floor. The rug between the armchairs and sofas, their bodies briefly reflected in the mirrors together with the whole room. Two pairs of lovers reeling down with all systems go.

'I always use the best, like ...' The voice cut out. A moan as he straddled and entered her. Then pitching and wild bucketing storm, rising, grappling, scratching, biting, kissing until they could not tell which was which and the rise seemed unending before it exploded in that moment of a thousand lights which rake over the bodies of lovers at their eternal five seconds of knowledge. A still-ness, followed by temporary separation.

'*Five G. CAP SEP green.*'
'*Roger. We read Capsule Separator is green.*'
'*Disarm. CAP SEP is green.*'
'*CAP SEP comes up.*'
'*CAP SEP is coming out ... and the turn round has started.*'
'*Roger. We read turn round started.*'
'*SCIP no movements.*'
'*Roger.*'
'*Okay, switching to manual pitch.*'
For a second time the floor became their bed. Hands touched and fingers probed. Their tongues became tiny flames of sensuality.
'*Manual pitch.*'
'*Pitch is okay. Switching to manual yaw.*'
The rugs, then the ceiling, yawed as they rolled. Neither could tell who was man or who woman.
'*Yaw is Okay. Switching to manual roll.*'
The roll was building into a second climax. A dizzy spin as the strength pulsed out of their bodies and they drifted on the warm air.
'*Roll is Okay.*'
'*Roll Okay. Looks good here.*'
'*On the periscope. View fine.*'
'*I'll bet.*'
'*Cloud cover over Florida. Clear and identify Andrus Island ...*'
They dressed in silence. Chicory, remembering Boysie's delights, changed her underwear. They dined at *Le Valois* off Madison Avenue, a favourite haunt of Chicory's. Gay, happy at their reunion. Boysie did not bother to go back to the Waldorf Astoria that night.

'Pity you can't stay for the rendezvous.' Boysie heard the voice as if from a distance. Like from Africa. 'Sorry?'
'I said it's a pity you can't stay for the rendezvous and

docking exercise. They've got four hours in orbit up there before the docking.' Birdlip gave him a strange look. 'Impressive isn't it?'

Boysie shook himself reluctantly from his strange suspended state. Birdlip had, almost telepathically, repeated something he had said to Chicory the night before. Now he found himself coming up with Chicory's reply.

'It's impressive all right.'

There was a lull. Indecision crackling around like a badly tuned transistor radio.

'Well, if you really must be getting back to New York.' Birdlip made motions as though shovelling snow away from a doorway to speed an unwelcome guest off the premises.

'I've got to get back to New York.' Boysie spoke like an educated parrot. It had all been too much. The trip to New York; meeting Chicory again, the crazy duet that followed; the journey to Cape Kennedy and, finally the launching.

In a highly anglicized manner Birdlip suggested that they should go and have a bite before Boysie's departure. Reluctantly, Boysie took a last glance around the Launch Control Centre and allowed himself to be hustled through the thick blast-proof doors.

Outside the blockhouse the stiff breeze which plucks consistently across the Cape hit them with a warm slap. Boysie stood still, eyes bulging, staring out over the landscape towards the extraordinary roadway which runs across Merritt Island from the huge Vertical Assembly Building up to the three launch pads of Complex Three Nine.

The roadway, lined with palmetto and streaked with blowing sand, consisted of two great strips of concrete slashing over the arid ground like some enormous motorway or a pair of giant runways designed for handling jumbo jets on some parallel system.

What really took Boysie's attention was the strange object which crawled along the road. It moved with the speed of a wounded insect; some hideous futuristic hybrid creature. A great squat structure crawling fantastically on, from what Boysie could see, eight caterpillar tracks. Atop the thick metal structure rose a tower of metal girders, quivering even at the snail slow place of the whole piece of apparatus: an umbilical tower for yet another rocket, a tall metal phallus twice the size of Nelson's Column shaking slightly as the breeze clipped away through the tower on to the unbelievable metal projectile.

'Quite a sight,' muttered Birdlip.

'The *Saturn V*?' Boysie did not need an answer.

'In the metal. Just about the most expensive piece of scrap you'll find around here.'

'And just the thing for whopping people up to the moon, eh?'

'Moon, June, croon, spoon . . .' chanted Birdlip heading towards his Landrover.

'Loon,' tried Boysie. 'When you have a base established up there think what a time the song writer'll have finding rhymes for *earth*.'

'Earth, mirth, curse, girth . . . Dearth?'

'Dearth is good.' They were in the Landrover now, engine started Boysie looked over his shoulder at the creeping crawling *Saturn V* transporter, the rocket that would ship men out over the oceans of space into the new world. The sky was now its familiar blue. High up a tiny straggle of cirrus made a small abstract pattern. The Landrover moved off towards lunch, brunch, munch whatever one had to eat at that time of day.

Birdlip began to chant:

> 'I look up at the earth,
> and chuckle with mirth,
> Because, like you, it has not lost its girth.'

37

Boysie smiled out of politeness and added:

'Yet my heart is full of dearth,
Because you have the . . .'

'Curse . . .' finished Birdlip.
'That was my line.' Boysie, sulkily.
'Okay. It was a lousy line anyway.'

In the canteen they sat down to bacon and eggs, over and easy, Birdlip lacing his with gouts of tomato sauce. The coffee was good.

Lighting his cigarette when the meal was done, Boysie quite suddenly felt the old sensation that all was not well. Someone seemed to be boring through the back of his neck with laser beam eyes.

Until then Boysie had, between bouts of exceptionally light banter with Rupert Birdlip, been indulging himself with offbeat thoughts about life in the real space age – *Make it Mars this Summer. Only £600 down and seven easy payments of £200 for the holiday of a lifetime. It's a kaleidoscope of colour; soft fragments of light fuse around you giving the most tender and enchanting background; the softest light and the sweetest music – music of the outer lands, and again that colour, gold, silver, crimson. The Lunar Hilton provides all. Six swimming pools, twelve bars, fully air conditioned, and here, folks, you can relax in complete safety without a helmet or pack. All this and television in every room, plus the freshest iced and pure water – transported for you and you alone. Luxuriate at the LUNAR HILTON.*

Then the eyes pricked the back of his neck. With as much graceful subtlety as he could muster, which meant a cumbersome scraping of his chair and a distinctly suspicious turning of the head, Boysie centred his eyes in the direction from which the sense of surveillance was coming. That he was being observed was not in doubt. The watcher sat alone at a table some twelve feet away, a man who could only be described as sparse. Slight, small, in his middle fifties, short cropped blond hair, narrow eyes which seemed huge behind a pair of very executive spectacles. For some odd reason, which Boysie could not pinpoint, the man reminded him of a weevil. It was probably the nose. In any case B. Oakes only knew about weevils because he was a subscriber to the *Time-Life Nature Library*.

'Who's that?' he grunted softly turning back to Birdlip.

'Who what?'

'That. Over my shoulder. Blond crew cut.'

'Oh Christ, don't say *he's* looking at us.'

'Observing not looking. He's been carving up the back of my neck with his eyeballs. Who is he? Mad Scientist?'

'Right on the button, baby. Let's get the hell out of here. That guy's hotter than a volcanic eruption when it comes to security and I'd like to keep this job. The hours suit Paula.'

'Who's Paula? I thought your wife's name was Janice.'

'It is. Paula's my twice a week girl with thighs. . . .'

'Like in the Playmate of the month. I know, I see them all the time.'

'Better. Smoother. Sort of more . . .'

'Caressable?'

'You might say that.'

'It still doesn't answer my question. Who's the nut?'

'Ellerman von Humperdinck. Doctor Ellerman von Humperdinck.'

'Spooky?'

'Sepulchrally. They say von Braun won't speak to him.'

'Perhaps it wasn't his department.' Boysie knew his Tom Lehrer.

'According to von Humperdinck they're all his departments.'

'Of German origin, I presume.' Boysie unfolded the last segment of the paper napkin in which his warm toast was wrapped, took the final piece and continued to practise the sin of gluttony.

'For Pete's sake move, that guy's toxic.'

'What makes him such a big wheel?'

'Hurry. He's a good rocket man but he's also very conscious of security. His background you know ...'

'No.'

'He worked at the Mittelwerke plant at Niedersachswerfen and the Russians got him. He was in on the first Russian-rocket, with Grottrup, Wolff, Albring and all that lot ...'

'The steppe deal.' Boysie frivolously.

'CIA finally got him out but he's always been a bit ...'

'Careful?'

'Please, Boysie, let's get ... Hell, he's coming over.'

Boysie could feel the man standing behind him, Birdlip was looking up, an imitation smile moulded on to his lips.

'Doctor von Humperdinck. Hi,' said Birdlip.

'Commander Birdlip. I am well thank you. And your friend?'

'He's well,' said Birdlip almost falling over himself in the rush.

'He looks well.' You could carve up the accent with a blunt razor blade. 'Introduce us, Commander.' He pronounced Commander with a K.

'Sure. Sorry. Doctor Ellerman von Humperdinck. Mr. Brian Oakes.'

'Ah so. And what do you do, Mr. Oakes? I like meeting new faces.'

Boysie was half standing, the attitude being one of near obeisance, trying desperately to follow the general method of Constantine Stanislavsky and willing his eyes to shine like neon.

'Not *the* Doctor von Humperdinck.'

'You have heard of me?'

'Who hasn't heard of you *Herr Doktor*?'

Humperdinck's almost genial attitude changed, the body stiffening like a child in a tantrum. The voice came out slipped: a Gestapo officer in an old movie.

'Doctor is my title. Herr Doktor is a title that has been sullied; I do not use it. Doctor is the rank bestowed upon me by my adopted country and we Americans must stick together, Mr. Oakes, don't you agree?'

'Certainly. I agree. But I'm from London so I'm biased.'

'You are not an American.'

'London, England. Buckingham Palace, the Changing of the Guard, Pall Mall, the Treasury by moonlight. Swinging.'

'So you are far from home. What are you doink in this neck of the woods?' He had a sharp little laugh and it was obvious that they were all expected to share the joke of a German rocket expert using outdated American slang. Both Birdlip and Boysie chuckled gently. An atmosphere of the rack and thumbscrews was never far from von Humperdinck.

'What am I doing here?' Boysie spoke with the assurance of a man in a minefield. 'Yes. What am I doing here? You'd better ask Commander Birdlip. I'm not quite sure how much I'm allowed to say.'

Birdlip was in there quick as a bird dog. 'Mr. Oakes has been out watching the launch. He's a rocket man as well.'

'Good. You specialize?'

The ball thudded firmly into Boysie's court. Luckily his recent space reading had stuck.

'My firm specializes. We're contracted to do some of

the gyroscopic work on the projected Aeroscope Flight Simulator.'

'Good. Very good. The LTV Simulator is excellent but we do need a more complex version. Much more complex.'

'So we understand.' Boysie was already treading water, hoping he would not get right out of his depth.

'Yes.' Von Humperdinck moved closer. Boysie tried to identify the after shave and finally plumped for *Ashes of Circus*. 'Between ourselves, a single-place gondola simulator is going to be outdated very quickly once we get the PRIME vehicles really going.'

'Yes. Yes. Of course.'

'And that will be sooner than you may think. It has been good meeting you, Mr. Oakes.'

Birdlip breathed out hard once von Humperdinck had departed.

'Lucky he didn't dig too deep.'

'Very,' said Boysie looking puzzled. 'Hey, what is PRIME?'

'Precision Recovery Including Manoeuvring Entry.' Birdlip spoke deadpan.

'Of course.' Boysie Oakes was lost. To him Precision Recovery Including Manoeuvring Entry suggested things obscene and delightful.

Boysie's trip back to New York from Melbourne, Florida, was moderately painless with the exception that he had been booked on one of the smaller airlines, the type that employs jokey pilots. The one on Boysie's flight did not excel in wit. 'Okay, folks, here we go for take off. Keep your prayer wheels turning and if anything happens don't forget to tell me.' 'If you look out of the left hand windows you can see my house. You missed it. Whoops, I didn't mean all of you look out of the left hand windows.' 'Did you know I was a cab driver before I took up flying these things? And I'm still not too hot on the U-turns.' 'Hey, guess what? I think the tail fell off. Oh, no it was just one of you overweight passengers going to the john.'

Boysie got back into Manhattan by late afternoon. Mostyn and Griffin were putting their feet up.

'Hail the conquering hero. There'll always be a lamp in the window for my wandering boy.' Mostyn giving Boysie a look reserved normally for erring waiters.

'Didn't go for a ride in one of them rockets then?' Griffin grinned.

'It was interesting, informative and ... er ... educational. Yes, educational's the word I would use.' Boysie grinned back.

Mostyn looked smug. 'While we're on the subject of your absence, hairy lad, what were you doing in an apartment up the street on Fifth Avenue the night before last? All night?'

Boysie crumpled fractionally, then regained his composure. 'None of your business.' That, he considered was the way to deal with the silky Mostyn. Then puzzled lines wrenched at his brow. 'How did you know anyway?'

'I've had occasion to warn you before, old darling. I have spies everywhere.'

Boysie saw the proverbial crimson. 'Oh, come off it, mate. You know your trouble? You've been over-specialized for too long. All you want is intrigue and tales of derring-do. Haven't they told you that era is long gone, man? Old 007, Nappy Solo and Dick Hannay are out of the charts. It's not cool to be in the cold anymore. The trend went out when *The Sunday Times* found out that Kim Philby was a fantasy dreamed up by the KGB.'

Mostyn held up his hand. 'Cease.' A small word but it had a well-honed edge the way Mostyn said it. 'No arguments, Oaksie. We have work.'

'Work?'

'An assignment.' Again the smug look.

'He means we bin hired.' Griffin from the safety of his chair.

'Who by?' Boysie was raiding the bar.

'By whom, lad, by whom. I've obviously failed to complete your education.'

'By whom?' Boysie sloshed the brandy into his glass.

'In general, the Universal Circle Shipping Company. In particular, Mr. Leo Warbash.'

'He means Mr. Warbash owns the Universal Circle Shipping Company,' explained Griffin noting the distressed look in Boysie's eye.

'The Universal Circle,' murmured Boysie taking a swift swig. 'Sounds like a group.'

'Boysie!' They all knew that tone of Mostyn's. It meant nix the frivolity. Mostyn put it into words. 'We can dispense with the humour. Mr. Warbash and his Universal Circle Shipping Company can mean a lot of nice dollars.'

'We're backing Britain,' mumbled Boysie.

'Right over the bluebirdshit-ridden cliffs of Dover,' joined in Griffin.

'Lots of dollars for us and the Treasury and, I understand, a free trip home by sea. No nasty frightening aeroplane rides, just the quiet thud of turbines and the warm sea breezes.'

Boysie turned, a shade vicious. 'Hoist the mainsail, belay there, bring in your bloody jibs.' He struck a pose intended to resemble the combined stances of Captain Bligh, Robert Newton playing Long John Silver and several unidentifiable actors having a go at Captain Queeg. 'I know that if you've fixed up something concerned with the sea it will be pretty bloody. Flaming Francis Chichesters we'll be, all wearing the Universal Circle Shipping Company badge instead of the Wool Mark. I know your games.'

'No games, Boysie.' Mostyn held up a hand in a conciliatory gesture. 'No games. We'll be getting all the information. It'll be like a cruise. Luxury, laddie. Can I never satisfy you?'

'Rarely.'

There was a soft tap at the door. The wood rapped gently by unmistakably feminine knuckles covered with soft material.

'That'll be the bint,' said Griffin ungraciously.

'The lady,' corrected Mostyn, crossing the room. 'I hope you approve of our choice, Boysie. GRIMOBO's American Rep.' He opened the door with a flourish. 'Come on in, darling. I think you've met the rest of the team. Mr. Brian Ian Oakes known commonly as Boysie . . .'

Chicory Triplehouse looked radiant. A black corduroy suit set off with a white blouse that was all but see-through. Boysie leaped across the room like a trained whippet, embracing her, whispering softly 'You didn't tell him did you?'

'What d'you think I am? We haven't met since 1964. Right.' Dead *sotto*.

'Right.' Boysie came up for air. 'Wow, it's good to see you. You get my vote.'

'If I might break up old home week for a moment.' Mostyn was trying to step between them like a censor scared for his own morals and to hell with how much the public could take.

'Spoil sport,' pouted Chicory.

'Yes, well, maybe. Only we have Mr. Warbash coming up in a few minutes and we don't want to give him any strange ideas do we?'

'Depends on what your corrupt little mind means by strange ideas.' Boysie turned back to Chicory. 'What in heaven's name made you want to work for a boss like this schnook, Chicory? He's pure venom and hambone broth, baby.'

'But you all work for him, sugar.' Doing her Southern belle bit. 'So I felt where my beau is that's where little old me ought to be.'

'Are you two always as nauseating as this?' Mostyn had taken Boysie's place at the bar.

'We're usually worse.' Boysie grinned smugly. 'Like a pop group gone religious. Anyway, what gives with Comrade Warbash? What's the score?'

'Wait and see little man, wait and see what I've fixed for us.'

Boysie turned to Griffin. 'So you tell me.'

Griffin hunched his shoulders, raising his hands, palms upwards. 'I know as much as you. Only the dirty grey chief here's got the information. 'Ent even met Warbash.'

Mostyn stepped into the middle of the room. 'To be honest, children, I do not know a great deal myself. The whole thing has to be cleared by Washington. I understand the CIA're involved. But, as far as I can make out, all that is required of us is that we act in a civilian capacity, hired by the Universal Circle Shipping Company, to protect their interests, during one journey on one of their ships, from the United States to Milford Haven. The four of us just sit on board and . . .'

'Four of us?' Boysie on the verge of a dream.

'Oh yes, we've got to give Miss Triplehouse some idea of how we run the British end of the business.'

'Of course,' said smiling Boysie locking eyes with Chicory who looked equally happy with the idea.

Griffin chuckled. Mostyn clothed himself with an air of modest disapproval and the telephone rang.

It was Reception announcing the arrival of Leo Warbash.

Mr. Leo Warbash's appearance was not unlike that of a sophisticated, intelligent, short, fat ape. A constant five o'clock shadow darkened his jowls, while his hairdresser

46

obviously had much trouble in controlling the black fleece which sprouted in floppy swirls, from his scalp. The same hair was repeated, in a minor form, on the podgy hands, right up his stubby little fingers, making them resemble large unpleasant spiders.

'Well, Washington's okayed it, Colonel Mostyn.' Warbash had the gruff voice of a self-made tycoon. The introductions were brief and to the point. A curt nod to Griffin, a flickering smile at Boysie, and an unashamedly expensive slaver towards Chicory.

'I think it would be best if you outlined the whole project to my colleagues.' Mostyn had the bland, fair manner of a huckster who knew the dice were loaded in his favour. 'I've really told them nothing as yet.'

'I see.' Warbash looked puzzled. 'I see. Okay, folks. I, er . . . where do I begin?' To Mostyn.

'At the beginning, Mr. Warbash. At the logical place.'

'Okay.' It was becoming apparent that Leo Warbash had a predeliction for the word 'Okay'.

'Well, as you know, my name's Leo Warbash. Leo Q. Warbash if you want it in full . . .'

'Wonder what the Q stands for . . .?' whispered Boysie into Chicory's silken ear.

'Quality,' mouthed back Chicory.

'I am the President of Universal Circle Shipping.' Warbash paused to allow the magnitude of the statement to hit them. 'We're not one of the giant companies but I guess we do okay. Ships in most areas, though I have to admit I felt kinda knocked out when the Government approached me on this present business.'

'It is *the business* we're interested in.' Boysie tried to jog him on.

'Yes. Yes, of course. Well up till about six years ago we simply operated freighters. Then I landed a sweet little contract and we branched out with three tankers. Oil tankers you understand.'

'Oil tankers,' repeated Griffin placidly to show he was still awake.

'Last year I bought another. Real dandy job. Had her re-registered the *Warbash Admiral* . . .'

'To cut the whole thing short,' Boysie was looking furiously towards Mostyn, 'we're all going to Milford Haven in an oil tanker.'

'A very modern vessel, Boysie. Like a luxury liner.'

'Even more modern by now, I reckon.' Warbash gave off pleased noises.

'Go on,' said Boysie grudgingly.

'A certain Government department, the name of which must remain secret . . .'

'I'll bet.' Again from Boysie.

'This department came to me with a contract which, quite frankly, gentlemen, I couldn't afford to refuse. Briefly I am required to move a cargo from the United States to Milford Haven, England, in the *Warbash Admiral*.'

'What's the cargo? Disc jockeys?' Boysie did not like what he was hearing.

'If you'll be patient. The whole operation is under the most strict security. The *Warbash Admiral* had to be taken straight into the Brooklyn Navy Yard for a special refit. My crew were given a most thorough security screening. I'm glad to say that Captain Bone, *Warbash Admiral's* original captain, will be in charge and most of her normal crew are on board. She sails tomorrow morning under sealed orders. But I can tell you that the cargo is to be picked up at a United States port before departure for Milford Haven.'

'And what do you want us for?' Boysie was downright belligerent by this time.

'That's just it.' Warbash laid a light easy smile on him. 'My board met to discuss the project a couple of days ago. They were all a little hung up on the security aspect of the job, we'd had a bit of trouble with insurance cover. Anyhow, even though the Government's putting three CIA men on board, my people felt that they would be primarily concerned with the Government's interest. What we wanted was some security to look after Universal Circle's interests.'

'So?'

'So I made some inquiries in Washington, got to hear about GRIMOBO and how you were over here . . .'

'And you offered us the job.'

'On the button.'

'And what's the cargo?'

'It's neither harmful nor live. That's all I can tell you.'

'Our fee, Boysie,' Mostyn as insidious as a plague virus, 'Our fee in this matter is one hundred thousand dollars.'

Boysie shut up quickly. He knew his values.

'So, gentlemen . . . I should say lady and gentlemen'. Warbash fired a salvo of leers at Chicory. 'Tomorrow morning I take it you will present yourselves at the Brooklyn Navy Yard, I have your permits here, to go on board the *Warbash Admiral* for "Operation Star".'

'Operation Star?' queried Griffin.

'It's not very imaginative but you know what governments are?'

Mostyn nodded sagely. 'Mr. Warbash has assured me,' he said sliding his eyes round the assembled members of GRIMOBO, daring dissent from any quarter, 'that our accommodation will be . . .'

'Superlative's the only word. And the little lady here need have no fears for her . . . her . . . er . . .'

'Honour?' tried Boysie.

'The little lady here's never had any fears about that,' said Chicory looking straight up Warbash's nose.

'Well, she'll be sleeping in the owner's cabin. Nothing but the best. My cabin's for you.'

'You did say you weren't coming on the trip yourself,

Mr. Warbash, didn't you?' Chicory kept her face straight.

'You'll have it all to yourself.' Warbash was uncompromisingly humourless.

Boysie allowed himself a quiet smile.

'I still don't like it.' Boysie continued to have a touch of the nagging worries.

Mostyn filled their glasses on Warbash's departure, now he sat brooding over the pile of papers the shipping man had left for them.

'What sort of cargo needs this kind of security if it isn't live or dangerous?' mused Boysie.

'Wish you'd stop soundin' off like a bleedin' crossword puzzle. Isn't a hundred thousand bucks enough?' Griffin was slightly put out, having proposed a visit to the *Latin Quarter* which was vetoed immediately on grounds of having to be fit and fresh for the job in the morning. At that point Boysie had facetiously mentioned that he would rather be fresh for this job that night. Chicory had gurgled and Mostyn made a remark which suggested that Boysie's mind never seemed to roam further than the night jollies.

'What's the size of this bloody ship anyway?' asked Boysie with some petulance, 'and no, one hundred thousand dollars isn't enough if my skin's going to suffer. I came into GRIMOBO on the strict understanding that we were going to do nice quiet jobs like looking through key holes and taking flash pictures of couples besporting themselves, not for skulduggery.'

Mostyn was shuffling through the papers. 'The *Warbash Admiral*.' He spoke almost to himself. 'It's largish. Gross tonnage around 60,000. Eight hundred feet long. A hundred and twenty-two feet across. Maximum speed sixteen knots. Twin diesels. Big bastard.'

'Had to have a major refit.' Boysie worried at it. 'Milford Haven? It couldn't be some new jet fuel could it? Milford Haven would have those facilities.'

'Could,' agreed Mostyn. 'On the other hand it could simply be something of a fair size. Something heavy. Milford Haven and Finnart are the only two British ports that can take the really heavy tankers. Anyway, we'll soon find out.' His voice held a hint of concern behind the steady manner. 'Let's drink to it. Here's to "Operation Star".'

They drank. Boysie shivered. He had that nasty premonition that he always associated with forthcoming disasters and terror which seemed to emanate from smooth Mostyn's unconcern. 'Operation Star,' he said gloomily.

CHAPTER THREE

SUPERCARGO

Rowing home to haven in sunny Palestine
With a cargo of ivory,
And apes and peacocks,
Sandalwood, cedarwood and sweet white wine.

CARGOES: John Masefield

BOYSIE still worried at the situation as he leaned over the rail of the observation platform on the forward part of the boat deck.

New York was slowly disappearing, going down with all hands off the starboard bow. If Boysie had been taking a home movie of the scene he would probably have made a note to back it with something by Gershwin. The Piano Concerto possibly. Boysie was pretty schmaltzy about NY, NY.

His original concern over the project was heightened when, once aboard the *Warbash Admiral*, it became apparent that nobody was going to do any talking or give them the full details of 'Operation Star'. Captain Bone, who turned out to belie his name, being a man of gross proportions, had welcomed them cordially enough, but made it plain that the contents of the sealed orders were not going to be publicly revealed until much later in the trip.

Mostyn in particular had not taken kindly to this; especially when three CIA agents, whom they immediately dubbed 'the three wise men', obviously knew all the details.

However, the GRIMOBO team began by having a social drop of the CIA boys, having been given the promised superlative accommodation — cabins normally inhabited by the owner and senior officers — on the boat deck.

In turn the CIA found themselves crammed into two cabins on the starboard side of the poop deck. This meant a twice daily climb to the boat deck for lunch and dinner with the GRIMOBO quartet in the owner's saloon.

Their first meeting was at lunch, when the CIA trio introduced themselves as Ed Frankenstein, Al Goldberg and Jimmy Meyer. Hence, the 'three wise men'. They all sat uneasy through the meal — cold Virginia ham with four kinds of salad, followed by strawberry flan — while Mostyn attempted to make conversation with Ed, Al and Jimmy. But they would not be drawn, departing rapidly once the last mouthful of coffee disappeared.

'The three bloody wise monkeys if you arsk me, not the wise bleedin' men,' commented Griffin.

'Certainly not forthcoming.' Mostyn was plainly niggled. 'I wonder if Chicory . . .?'

'Oh, no.' Boysie was in there with flailing words to defend the amorous Miss Triplehouse. 'I'm not letting Chicory do any of the Mata Hari stuff.'

'Oh, Boysie,' snuggled Chicory, part pleased, half put out.

'All we need to know at this stage,' pondered Mostyn, detached, 'is the nature of the cargo.'

So, now, from his vantage point on the boat deck, Boysie quietly checked through the visible alterations which had been made to the ship.

The superstructure seemed to have remained unharmed, pushed, as it was, to the rear of the ship. Above him was the nerve centre, the captain's deck and the navigation deck. Below were the poop and lower bridge decks, then the number one deck which led into the, presumably empty, bowels of the ship.

The great long deck, which swept away below the superstructure, seemed to have been cleared of the apparatus which formerly would have marked the vessel as a floating oil conveyor. The usual nest of pipes, which run, fore and aft, down the centre of the deck, had been removed, together with the big mobile gantry which normally spreads its jungle of metal girders across and above the deck, athwartships.

There was also no sign of the myriad small hatches which segment the main deck of a tanker. Instead, the deck seemed to have been re-built, a hairline crack showing that it had now become a pair of vast doors which would open from the centre. Impatient, Boysie desperately wanted to know what lay below that huge hatchway. That, at least, might provide a clue to their future cargo.

The sea was black satin, waveless, as still as the grave; and the ship seemed strangely silent, only the crushing thud of its twin diesels and the splash of the ocean against its heavy metal sides betrayed the fact of life within. Boysie moved himself to the rear of the deck and stepped quietly up the companionway which led to the hatch. There seemed to be little sign of life on the poop deck, so he followed the stairs down through the lower bridge deck on to the main deck. Here there was life, male marine life calling, echoing and singing to each other.

'Abaft. Belay there ye rabble.' Boysie mouthed silently. 'Back to the fo'c's'le ye lily-livered swabs. Har-har.' Aloud he said, 'Good evening,' to a cook who appeared to be going on duty.

'And good evening to you, too, ducky,' replied the cook.

Boysie returned to the task in hand: getting into the area which had once housed gallons of oil. There was only one forward companionway which seemed to lead downwards. For a second Boysie wondered if he should go back and get a ball of string to trail in his wake. Then he began the long descent. The narrow stairs seemed to go on for ever, twisting at regular intervals, until he thought there was a distinct probability of ending up bang in the middle of old Father Neptune's tea party. This set a train of thought going on to the more lustful and basic functions of man when faced with mermaids. He reached the final steps without having solved the problem of how and where. 'Very tricky things, mermaids,' breathed Boysie.

The steps had brought him into a small metal area, from which two passages spread out at angles moving forward. It was the way Boysie wanted. He entered the right hand passage and could see that it ended, some ten yards away, in a heavy bulkhead door. He had about six paces to go when the all too familiar pricking sensation rippled up the back of his neck. A second later the voice said, 'Lost your way, Charlie?'

Boysie turned to find Jimmy Meyer, all six foot two of him, leaning against the passage wall, one hand lazily draped inside his jacket.

'No. Course not. It's okay.' Boysie thought he sounded undismayed. He turned and took another step towards the bulkhead door.

'Hold it.' Meyer pronounced the words nice and easy, prolonging the 'ho' of hold.

'Look. I've got a job to do.'

'Haven't we all, Charlie? Mine is guarding the bulkhead doors here and letting nobody through.'

'And mine is going to have a look-see. I am employed by the owner after all . . .'

'So you're employed by the owner. The owner has nothing to do with it. This ship is on government business and the Central Intelligence Agency is in charge of all security aspects.'

Boysie moved back and stood close to him, as though measuring up. They were both about the same size and weight. Not that Boysie had any intention of tangling with the man.

'Now look.' Meyer smiled. 'We don't want any upsets. Why not just go back to your cabin and rest up before dinner.'

'You mean you don't recognize our position on board this ship?'

'You asking or telling?'

'Both.'

'Well the answer's yes on each count, sentences to run concurrently.'

Stalemate. Boysie gently gnawed the side of his lower lip and looked up at Meyer, sly with a lot of white showing and the pupils right up in the right hand corners. Cornered cornea. Then, quickly, as though he had made his mind up on a whim, Boysie took off with a light 'Okay'. He trotted easily to the far end of the passage. At the foot of the steps he turned.

'Hey!' Boysie shouted back to Meyer. 'What about the Bay of Pigs then?'

Meyer flapped a hand. A move-on-there gesture. Boysie's foot was on the first step when Meyer thought of a retort.

'What about Kim Philby?'

'I'm sorry but they're quite within their rights.' Captain Bone faced Mostyn and Boysie across his desk. He looked more than a little embarrassed. Mostyn had exploded wrathfully when Boysie told him about the show of CIA strength. But his tidy military mind allowed that their only way to recognition lay through the Captain. So, within twenty minutes of leaving Meyer, Boysie found himself in the Captain's cabin.

'This is monstrous, Captain, absolutely monstrous.' Mostyn was doing his practised imitation of a British senior officer, *circa* 1939, curry hot and peevish. It was just this kind of action that might bring Bone to his knees, or at least the fatty centres of his legs which passed for such. But Bone just did not have the authority.

'To be fair with you, Colonel Mostyn, I begged Mr. Warbash not to put you aboard. The whole operation is government controlled as you can see. Yesterday I asked for permission to tell everyone once we were at sea. The orders came back very firm. I'm not to say a word until we've picked up the cargo and are at sea again.'

'It's ludicrous.'

'I kinda agree with you. In a couple of days you'll see the cargo coming aboard anyhow. And I've already got a large percentage of the crew who know.'

Mostyn made an ugly sneezing sound.

'So my hands are tied,' the Captain continued. 'I'd really appreciate it if you just sat back and enjoyed yourselves.' He chuckled uneasily. 'Let the CIA play James Bond, eh?'

But Mostyn's pride was hurt. Boysie watched him before dinner that night, brooding, the angry look on his face almost screaming details of the plot which was certainly thickening in his mind.

Before the CIA men arrived for dinner, Mostyn drew Boysie to one side.

'Don't say anything to the others.' He muttered with secret sotto into Boysie's ear. 'Just wait. We'll get the bastards tomorrow. Come and see me then.'

Boysie nodded like a trained dog. For his part the whole business had now become farcical, even though he still felt the inevitable uneasiness and worry. What the hell, thought Boysie. So we don't know what the cargo's going to be. We'll know in a couple of days and to blazes with the CIA. Who cares anyway?

Meyer did not appear with Goldberg and Frankenstein for dinner.

'He'll be up later,' Goldberg told them laconically.

Frankenstein eyed Chicory with blatant lasciviousness throughout the meal, while the whole of the GRIMOBO team ate through the menu in silence.

'Like a lot of kids,' observed Boysie later, in the soothing confines of the owner's cabin.

'Well let's make this a bit adult, darling.' Chicory's voice came smooth as satin pants in the darkness that surrounded them. 'Lifebuoy may not like BO but I do.'

On the following morning, Boysie presented himself at Mostyn's cabin. Mostyn had about him the wicked aura of a child ready to practise evil.

'That's our answer, little Boysie.' Mostyn held up a small medicine bottle.

'I'm supposed to say, what dat, presumably.'

'Indeed. And I answer in one word. Jalap.'

'Jalap?'

'That's it, Oaksie, old love. Jalap.'

'What dat?'

'Something from my survival kit.' Mostyn brim full of malice. 'Jalap is a particularly powerful purgative. They don't seem to use it much nowadays, but when I was a small boy . . .'

'Purgative.' Boysie mused. Some words seemed to have been permanently left out of his vocabulary.

Mostyn sighed and flicked some imaginary ash from his finely pressed slacks. 'A purgative. Or, if it makes it any easier, a laxative . . .'

'Oh, it makes you sh . . .'

'It is obtained, I gather, from the tuber of a Mexican plant.'

'Tuba? The Tijuana Brass again, hu?'

'Tuber. B-E-R.'

'Cut. Look, daddy, I've had trouble with Mexican juices before. You remember the mushroom soup in Berlin?'

'Well.' An affirmative from Mostyn. 'Yes I remember

it well, Oakes. But this tiny tincture has nothing to do with mushrooms, hallucinatory or otherwise.'

'So what's it do apart from making you sh . . .?'

'That's all it does. Few drops of this stuff, Boysie, and you could move a four months' constipated elephant in fifteen minutes flat, and he would stop to remember.'

'That powerful, eh?'

'More. This is the answer to every bunged up bowel in the business. And if you aren't bunged up its effect is catastrophic.'

Boysie looked hard at the small bottle and then at Mostyn. 'Perhaps I'm dim, but I don't see the connection.'

'You are as dim as a red light on Knob Hill. The connection is that the CIA performs the changing of the guard directly after dinner.'

'How come you know that?'

'I took the trouble to follow them last night. I rather gather they keep up the watch round the clock. Goldberg relieved your friend Meyer after dinner last night. I've just seen him with Meyer this morning which means that Frankenstein is on duty now. He'll probably be relieved after lunch and, in turn, tonight after dinner they'll go through the routine again.'

'And?'

'And, Boysie, my dear oaf, the one who takes over after dinner tonight will be spiked.' Mostyn paused for it to register. 'Spiked. Full of Jalap, friend. Jalap which we feed into him over the merry festive board . . .'

'How?' Boysie was determined to be as cagey as possible with any plan concocted by Mostyn.

'What do they drink?'

'Can't say I've noticed.'

'Well I have. They're strictly soda pop boys. No booze on duty. Not even a small carafe of harmless rosé, my rosy lad. One coke each which they actually drink with their food.'

'Ah.'

'They must have palates like hardboard.'

'So we spike the cokes.' Boysie grinned, another infant joining Mostyn's childhood jape.

'We do, indeed. I've checked that as well. The steward keeps the freezer stacked up. Just before every meal it contains twelve cokes, twelve cans of beer, and four bottles of a rather inferior Burgundy: two white and two red. Before dinner tonight we move in, prise the caps off the coke bottles, insert a brace of drops in each bottle and push the caps on again.'

'And what if I want a coke?'

'You won't.' Mostyn shook his head hard. 'Tonight coke'll be the last thing you'll want. And keep the others off it as well.'

'How quick do you say this stuff works?'

'We'll give it between twenty minutes and half an hour. Yes about half an hour after they've taken it.'

'Hope they don't linger over the meal.'

'They haven't up to now.'

'There's always a first time, not that I'd mind being around when it happens.'

'Yes, well you won't be, will you?' Mostyn cocked his head on one side.

'No.' Boysie got the message. 'What you mean is that I'll be risking life and limb going down to have a peek into the hold and hoping that the CIA bird-dog will be trapped in the loo.'

'Couldn't have summarized it better myself, lad.'

So it turned out that half an hour before dinner that evening Boysie and Mostyn crept into the boat deck saloon. Mostyn poured a couple of brandies from his hip flask and they began the tricky job of systematically removing the caps from the dozen bottles of coke neatly packed into the bar freezer. The operation took them fifteen minutes. Caps prised off. Two drops of jalap inserted into each bottle. Caps on again and made tight with a pair of household tweezers. Up, up and away.

Shortly before dinner they were joined by the other two members of GRIMOBO in the saloon, followed, minutes later, by Goldberg and Frankenstein who made straight for the freezer and the coke.

'That's a good idea.' It was Griffin who broke the silence in an attempt to be friendly. 'You boys've got something. I really fancy a coke tonight.'

Mostyn flashed a look at Boysie which said, 'Didn't you warn him?'

Boysie's look in return was a sombre, 'No.'

By this time, Griffin was already lifting his glass, in toast to the pair of CIA men, quaffing the liquid with much smacking of lips.

Mostyn turned his head away so that nobody would see his lips moving surreptitiously. 'It's not such a bad thing, Boysie. They won't be so suspicious if one of our people goes down with the dreaded bug as well.'

Boysie nodded and they took their places for the meal. The conversation remained as sporadic as ever, Goldberg and Frankenstein hurrying through their food like a couple of convicts on release morning. Within a quarter of an hour the two Americans nodded politely to Chicory, Mostyn, Boysie and Griffin, and headed for the door.

'We've only got to hope that comrade Meyer gets up here fully relieved before either of them needs relief,' muttered Mostyn.

'Watch old Griff,' said Boysie.

They chatted amiably for five minutes or so. Then Meyer arrived looking irritable. He had barely taken his place at the table when Griffin let out an oath.

'Christ,' said Griffin loudly.

'You all right?' asked Chicory.

'Whatsmatter, old son?' queried Mostyn.

'Something you ate?' Boysie chirped.

'Cor, me guts.' Griffin was doubled up in his chair. 'Cor. Screamin' hell. Cor.' Still bent double, he made a swift exit.

'That walk,' commented Mostyn ruthlessly, 'reminded me of Charles Laughton playing Quasimodo.'

'Better see if he's okay,' said Boysie lightly.

'Yes. Mind you, I think old Griff is a shade faster than Laughton was.' Mostyn could have been perfectly serious.

On the boat deck observation platform all was still and quiet. A silence more penetrating than that of the previous afternoon when Boysie's initial reconnaissance had been aborted. In fact the silence now seemed to permeate the whole ship. Boysie began his journey down to the hold. Silence everywhere. A ghost ship? No, there was the usual crew noise coming from number one deck. Boysie used the same route down. Towards the bottom of the stairs he was conscious that the engine noises became louder. Now they were accompanied by low groans which seemed to be coming from the metal walls of one of the passages leading to the heavy bulkhead doors of the hold.

Boysie crept forward. The groans increased in volume. He could now pinpoint their position. They came from behind a three-quarter companionway door set in the wall of the passage. The door was neatly labelled *Crew Toilets*.

'The jalap goes around and around, oh-oh-oh, and it comes out here,' warbled Boysie softly, making for the bulkhead door.

The handle was heavy and difficult to move, but after a couple of heaves it came up with a hard metallic click. Slowly Boysie pushed the bulkhead door which opened easily. A moment later he stepped through into a blaze of arc lights and a hold which looked twice the size of the Albert Hall. Several men were working about a hundred yards away and Boysie only had time for a quick glimpse of the main features before a thick-necked, bull-like seaman turned and saw him. There was a second of indecision, then a cry of 'Intruder'.

All hell broke loose with the ringing of alarm bells. In momentary panic, quite reasonable when one considered that three seamen with the physiques of heavyweight champions, were fast heading in his direction, Boysie took off and hoofed it for the companionway.

Going up was always more difficult than coming down, but Boysie negotiated the turns in the stairs like a mountain goat. His mind was reacting like a mountain goat's as well. Sheer self preservation sent him whipping up to the boat deck in the manner of a speeded-up silent movie. He didn't stop until he was inside Mostyn's cabin.

Mostyn looked up from his book. 'Must you make all that noise?'

'I've ... hah ... I've ... hah ... whoo ...' Boysie struggled to get words out through the laboured breathing

'You smoke too much, laddie. Your wind's gone.' Mostyn was stretched out on his bunk fully clothed and with a copy of *The Wind in the Willows* which he was nonchalantly trying to hide.

'I've ... whoo ... been ... hah ... with you ... hah ... all the ... evening ... hah ... right?'

'Not if your breathing hasn't improved by the time someone comes to ask, Oaksie. They'll think it thumping strange if you've been with me all night and you're sitting at the table there acting like a landed trout.'

'Tell ... hah ... them it's my ... hah ... asthma.'

'Get quietly knotted, boy. You nearly got caught, didn't you?'

There was a banging at Mostyn's door. He slid the copy of *Wind in the Willows* down the side of his bunk, nicely out of sight.

'I'll tell Griff and Chicory what your ... hah ... bedtime reading is ... hah ... if you don't ... hah ... alibi me ... whoop,' Boysie hissed out.

Mostyn opened the cabin door. A young officer stood there; behind him two hard seamen were having a lurk.

'Yes?' asked Mostyn sounding like a dowager duchess about to fob off some tradesman pressing for his bill.

'Sorry to bother you, sir, but we're trying to account for passengers' movements during the last half an hour. I wondered...'

'Passengers,' shrieked Mostyn, 'I'm not a bloody passenger, man. Neither's my colleague here. Mr. Oakes. We're both employed by the firm that pays *you*.'

'Yes, sir, I know but...'

'But me no buts, lad. Anyway, Mr. Oakes and myself have been discussing our company policy since dinner.'

'I see, sir.' The officer looked dissatisfied. 'You wouldn't know where the occupant of number three cabin is would you, sir? A Mr. Griffin?'

'Griffin? Isn't he in his cabin?'

'We aren't getting any answer.'

'Well go in and try the bathroom. He's not too well. You'll nose him out somehow I'm sure. What's the panic anyway?'

'Slight breach in security, sir. Nothing difficult.'

'Glad to hear it.' Mostyn had the door closed before the man could answer. He stood for a moment with his ear to the ventilation grille until he was satisfied the party had left. Then he turned to face Boysie.

'You got your lungs under control yet?

'Fine thanks. Fine.'

'Well, what the hell happened?'

Boysie gave Mostyn a brief résumé of the incident. Mostyn looked thoughtful, then asked 'Did you see *anything*?'

'Oh yes. Quite a bit. They've completely stripped the

interior. The roof, that would be the underside of the main deck, looks as though it's been strengthened. I should imagine it opens with two leaves moving out and away from each other. There looked to be at least six hydraulic jacks along each side.'

'They've cleared all the tanks out?' Mostyn leaned forward in interest.

'The lot. Now there's a row of great metal cradles going right up the centre.'

'Cradles?'

'Big, half-circular things. From what I could see they stand on two legs, pivoted at the centre of the cradle. The legs are clamped to the deck and there are a couple of dirty great springs running from each side of the cradle to the deck.'

'Stabilizers.'

'I suppose so.'

'How many? How many cradles?'

Boysie raised his eyes. 'You're joking. I was only in there a few seconds. Reckon I did bloody well.'

'Better than nothing.' Mostyn was admiring himself in the mirror. 'But what does it tell us?' He asked with a mind on his receding hairline rather than the cargo.

'Dunno.' Boysie looked blank. 'Some bloody great aeroplane fuselage I suppose.'

'A rocket?' Mostyn turned. A schoolmaster confronting the class.

'Why take a rocket to the UK? We haven't got any launch sites for one thing.'

'The ship would take a rocket though?'

'I reckon so but . . .'

'One of the big ones?'

'Yea. But . . .'

'Let's wait and see. I wasn't so worried about the cargo. We've put one over on the CIA that's the main thing, lad. Well done. Well done.'

'Bloody schoolboy tricks,' said Boysie, not quite loud enough for Mostyn to hear.

Goldberg and Frankenstein did not make an appearance at lunch on the following day, even though the *Warbash Admiral* had changed course and was now moving steadily along the coastline which came into view around eleven-thirty.

Griffin returned to the fold soon after one in the afternoon, while Mostyn, Boysie and Chicory were leaning over the boat deck rail watching the activity which seemed to have suddenly activated the crew.

'Feeling better, old lad?' asked Mostyn giving Boysie one of his special roguish digs in the ribs.

'Cor. Don't want a go like that again,' said Griffin. 'Like a fleet of little minesweepers doing an operation on me guts. Terrible.'

'A bug, I expect.' Boysie, with one arm round Chicory, grinned.

'Gather two of our CIA friends caught it as well,' crooned Mostyn.

'Oh. Is that why they weren't at lunch?' cooed Chicory who had been let into the secret. 'I saw Mr. Meyer just now in the saloon. He looked terribly tired.'

'Hey,' chipped in Boysie. 'Is it my imagination or are we moving inshore?'

'Hand me the telescope,' muttered Mostyn.

The four watched as slowly the coastline changed. First, from a blue-grey blobby line into a more clearly defined land mass. They came closer and Boysie began to get the feeling that he had been there before. A spit of land jutted into the sea and, as they approached, one could make out strange skeletal shapes and geometric lines of white buildings.

'Cape Kennedy,' said Boysie.

'No?' Mostyn mocked. 'We thought it was one of your

66

beloved firework factories what with all those rockets. Wake up, lad, we've been looking at them for the past hour.'

'Then we're going to Port Canaveral. You might be right. A rocket.'

Mostyn looked at Boysie with the expression of one who is tired of holding his temper. 'You doubted me?'

'Well . . .'

'Doesn't do to have doubts about your uncle Mostyn, lad. Should've thought you'd have learned by now that when I say turn . . .'

'We all turn,' chorused the others.

'Quite,' said Mostyn.

They tied up in Port Canaveral just before two-thirty, and for the next three hours the GRIMOBO team, now joined by the CIA trio, watched the incredible scene as the *Warbash Admiral* was loaded with her supercargo.

The cargo itself lay placid in three sections on low rail trucks by the dockside. Three long, huge cylindrical objects, cocooned in what looked like a soft grey rubber.

The ship vibrated slightly as the whole deck opened up from the centre, the long hatch gently lifted by hydraulic jacks leaving the ship ripped open and exposing its entrails.

Down the centre of this great metal womb ran the line of cradles, arms reaching up to embrace the cylinders. Next followed the slow and precise business of winching each section up and on the creaking gantry crane which had slid into position, bridging the ship.

Then the lowering, so that the cylinder dropped gently into place, held securely by the cradle arms. After this the upper sections of the cradle had to be swung out, piece by piece, lowered, and clamped into position.

It was just before six o'clock that the technicians waved to the bridge and the hydraulic jacks came into play again, sealing off the *Warbash Admiral*'s innards.

At six-thirty the diesels started up, and, within the hour, they were at sea once more. At ten, the public address system crackled into life. By this time Boysie was snug in Chicory's cabin, but the Captain's voice held off pleasure.

'This is your Captain speaking. Captain Bone. I am now authorized to inform all of you that, having opened the sealed orders under which we are sailing, we are making all possible speed to Milford Haven, England. Our cargo is, as most of you will have already gathered, a *Saturn V* rocket, together with an Apollo capsule. We are on a very special mission. One that all Universal Circle personnel should be proud to be concerned with . . .'

'Get on with it,' muttered Boysie.

'Doing what I can, darling, but you're not helping much,' smooched Chicory.

'Not you. Cap'n Flint up there.'

The Captain was still telling the Universal Circle personnel that this was their special way of serving the country they loved and its President.

'It's not very nice is it?' said Chicory. 'Like being watched by someone you can only hear.'

'The object of *"Operation Star"* is purely peaceful and to maintain the bond of friendship between the peoples of the United States and Great Britain . . .' continued Bone.

'It says here,' commented Boysie.

'This *Saturn* rocket and Apollo capsule will be taken to London, there to be displayed as a memorial to the achievements of the United States Space Administration.'

'Silly twits. A whole *Saturn V* on display in London. There'll be protest marches all over the place.'

There was a tap at the door and Mostyn walked in.

'Yow,' cried Chicory, covering herself.

'Hey, you can't just walk in . . .'

'Never mind about that,' said Mostyn. 'Just keep still while I'm talking to you.' He looked at the couple with disgust. 'You heard that?'

'Mmm.' Boysie and Chicory shook their heads affirmatively.

'Good. Well you'll realize that we must play our part in seeing the wretched thing gets safely to Milford Haven. No more mucking about with the CIA chaps and . . .'

'It was you that did the mucki . . .'

'AND,' Mostyn bellowed, 'be on your guard. Constantly. Right?'

'Right,' repeated Boysie and Chicory.

'Be on your guard,' repeated Boysie when Mostyn left. 'Who the hell wants a bleeding great piece of space hardware like a *Saturn V*. Everyone knows the details. Anyway. Me, I'm for an enjoyable cruise.'

CHAPTER FOUR

SWITCH

The commonest and cleanest cold-deck switch is pure sleight of hand. The sharper slips the cold deck out of his pocket into his lap. Drawing the pack on the table towards him for the deal, he drops it tidily into his lap, in the same motion snapping the cold deck into its place at the table's edge.

SCARNE ON CARDS

BOYSIE never really knew what sea sickness was until their third day at sea after leaving Port Canaveral. The nagging jitters now lay behind him. What was there to fear from a docile *Saturn V* asleep in the hold? Time now to relax and get that sea cruise feeling. Time also to sensuate with Chicory. The next few days seemed bright and beautiful.

Then, on the second night, Captain Bone ordered all moveable gear to be lashed down, warning them that the *Warbash Admiral* would be passing through some 'choppy water' during the early hours and most of the next morning.

To begin with it was not too bad. Boysie following his usual routine, left Chicory's cabin around four in the morning, and made his way around the boat deck observation platform, back to his own cabin.

He had just slid into the welcoming bunk when the first choppiness hit them. He slept, however, and even ate the breakfast brought by a chirpy steward in the morning.

The trouble began when he tried to get up. Boysie

swung his feet on to the floor just as the ship bucked slightly. His head reeled without warning, while a preliminary rush of nausea hit his guts. The only answer was to stretch out on the bunk again and groan – with feeling.

Around noon, Boysie attempted to rise for the second time. He staggered, half-dressed, through the companionway on to the observation platform which, by this time, seemed as stable as a roller coaster. The sea was not running unduly high, but Boysie had the unpleasant sensation of being pitched about at an alarming angle.

On looking back, he seemed to recall seeing other ships bearing down upon them out of a less distracted sea. A head-cleaving pain ploughed into the core of his brain and he felt the nausea begin its vertical rise.

Sweating heavily, and anxious not to make a public exhibition of himself, Boysie wrenched his way to the cabin and into his bathroom. He even managed to lock the door before giving himself up to the miserable whirling world of sea sickness. Through it all he imagined that he could hear voices calling outside. The bathroom spun. Stomach corkscrewed. There was something unusual about the ship's stability. His whole digestive tract was being turned inside out. Colour. Blotches of brilliant colour flashing on and off against the shower curtain. More nausea. Retching. Oh God, I want to die. Retch. Oh. Retch. Colours. Pounding in the head. Someone was running up a jet engine inside the skull. Retch. Pain. Colour.

It was a good hour and a half before Boysie returned to what might be termed a right state of mind.

Weak, and still miserable, he washed, groped his way into the cabin, put on a shirt and slacks and then made his way on to the observation platform for a much needed breath of fresh air. They were moving quite fast, the sea now flattened and calm.

'Hold it. Stand perfectly still.' The voice came, authoritatively, out of nowhere. Boysie whirled towards it.

71

Standing well forward on the observation platform was a tall young man in the uniform of the United States Marine Corps.

'Now look . . .' Boysie began, puzzled. He had not seen any Marines on board before.

'No looks about it, buddy. Just come up to me. Come slow and easy like.'

Boysie decided that it was best not to argue. Especially as the Marine was holding an M15 carbine with the wicked eye of its muzzle staring unblinkingly at Boysie's uneasy stomach.

The events which placed Boysie in his new predicament had begun shortly before noon. Mostyn was now in the habit of visiting Captain Bone around the noon hour, the Captain having a very superior brand of whisky at his disposal.

Mostyn was never sick at sea. Or if he was, he made certain nobody knew about it. Just before midday, he was holding forth, at some length, on the psychological facets of seasickness, when the Captain's squawk box let out its nervous raspberry.

'Captain here.' Bone pressed the speak button while Mostyn lapsed into an aggravated silence. James George Mostyn disliked being interrupted, especially by a gadget.

'Bridge here, sir. Officer of the watch. Three vessels and helicopter escort approaching us. Bearing Red, three-three-zero.'

'Military vessels?'

'Look like ocean-going cutters, sir. Like the *Dallas*, *Hamilton* and *Sherman*.'

'Out this far?'

'That's what they look like, sir.'

'Okay, I'm coming up.' The Captain rose. 'Seems we got company. Care to join me on the bridge, Colonel?'

Mostyn nodded his thanks and followed the bulky Captain out of his cabin, marvelling at the way in which he swung his large girth around with such ease in so small and confined an area.

The officer of the watch turned out to be the young man who had disturbed Mostyn while he was sheltering Boysie on the night of the jalap. 'They're over there, sir.' He spoke rapidly to the Captain, pointing towards the three growing blobs scurrying towards them off the port beam. The blobs gave off white spews of foam as they pressed forward. Above them a brace of helicopters maintained station.

Bone lifted his binoculars. 'You're right. I think they are ocean-going cutters. Yes. Flying the Stars and Stripes. Hang on . . .'

A light began to flash intermittently from the leading craft. Their form was now quite distinguishable. Long rakish fast ships clipping through the water and looking as tough as they come.

'Can you read what they're flashing?' The Captain turned to the young officer.

'Whisky Zebra, Whisky Zebra, Whisky Zebra,' read the officer of the watch.

'Our security call sign.' Bone dropped the information to Mostyn. 'Signal back Whisky Zebra.'

One of the helicopters had broken away from the main formation now and was descending towards the tanker. Bone pulled open the port sliding door of the bridge and leaned out, looking towards the helicopter's hatchway. One hand came up holding a pistol-grip power megaphone.

'Hear this, Captain. Hear this.' The voice echoed strangely above the engine and wave noises.

Captain Bone waved an arm in assent.

'Request permission to land small detachment United States Marines aboard you.' The voice went on, poised above them. 'Complete radio silence still to be observed. We have information of possible saboteurs among your crew.'

Bone turned back on to the bridge. 'Signal them to come aboard.' His face was a nasty shade of grey. Mostyn looked out across the water. During the last few minutes they had slid from the roughish water into comparatively calm sea. The leading ship was closing on them, coming alongside.

'Stop engines,' commanded Bone.

The officer of the watch clanged down on the engine room control handle. Mostyn glanced towards the segmented indicator and saw the needles pointing to STOP ALL ENGINES. The diesel thud, to which they were all acclimatized, slowed, faltered, and then stopped. Now all the other noises seemed suddenly magnified: the buffeting of the wind, chug of helicopter engines and the sounds coming from the ocean-going cutter now only a short distance from them.

'Pipe all hands of the port watch to assist visitors coming aboard.' The officer of the watch spoke into the bridge microphone. Within seconds a voice echoed the command on the loudspeaker system. Men began to appear, ready to lash the two ships together.

The helicopter dropped steadily towards the deck forward of the bridge. A rope ladder coiled and snaked from the hatch, and a small figure descended. Then another, and another, until seven Marines stood on the metal deck.

From the bridge, Mostyn could see that the party was made up of two officers and five enlisted men. They disappeared into the superstructure and arrived on the bridge two minutes later, minus three of the enlisted men. All wore the olive drab of battle order, the enlisted men equipped with M15 carbines and the two officers carrying unholstered automatics.

74

The senior, a major with large ears and red hair, advanced unerringly towards Captain Bone and saluted.

'Major Bernard, United States Marine Corps.' There was a trace of what Mostyn called yucky-hick in the man's voice.

'What's the score, Major?' Bone stood as though welded to the bridge deck.

'Sorry to cause you delay, Captain, but Lieutenant Gladzinsky here, and myself, have orders to inspect all persons on board. We have descriptions of two who may be among your crew. Suspect saboteurs.'

'Who the hell'd want to sabotage this ship?'

Gladzinsky, who was a small bouncy pink-cheeked young officer, grinned evilly. 'Not so much the ship as the cargo, Captain.'

'Yea,' drawled the Major. 'So could you muster all hands. I've got more men coming aboard.' His eyes looked past Bone's left shoulder towards the large cutter which was now secured to the port side of the *Warbash Admiral*. Scrambling nets had been hauled up and a steady stream of Marines were clambering up the swaying side, over the rails and on to the deck. Mostyn noted that they all seemed excellently drilled, each group of men moving rapidly into what looked like a predetermined position.

Bone stared thoughtfully at the Major. 'Okay,' he said at last, 'I'll order all hands to boat stations.'

'That'll be just fine.' Gladzinsky spoke in a menacing manner. The manner of a traffic cop who knew he had got you on toast.

'Hear this. Hear this.' The officer of the watch was speaking into the bridge microphone, this time linked directly to the loudspeaker system. 'All hands to boat stations. Prepare to abandon ship.' He clicked the main switch into the off position and smiled towards the Captain. 'That ought to make them move, sir.' Already there

75

was the noise of feet running on the decks below them.

'Good. Very good,' said the Major. 'I liked the prepare to abandon ship bit. It . . .' He was interrupted by the arrival of a Marine sergeant. The sergeant seemed opposed to the disciplinary habit of saluting. He simply cocked his head back towards the companionway and spoke off-handedly to the Major.

'The radio room's out of action. One guy got a bit tough so we had to put him out. They'll have to carry him off . . .'

'What the hell . . .?' Bone reacted violently, moving aggressively towards Major Bernard. But his way was blocked by the Major's automatic.

'You must learn to control your tongue, Spider.' The Major spoke over his shoulder to the sergeant who was now intent on lighting a cigarette. 'We hadn't let the Captain into our surprise yet.'

Mostyn took a pace forward, his hand automatically going for the pistol which was not there.

'Down, boy.' Gladzinsky grinned his evil grin again. Mostyn stopped with the sudden appreciation that there was a fair amount of fire power directed at them.

'What is this?' Bone's voice quiet, controlled with no hint of anxiety.

'Well,' the Major smiled. 'Some folks might call it piracy . . .'

'On the high seas,' added Gladzinsky.

'Like he says. On the high seas.'

'And just what do you intend to do to my men?'

'Not just your men, Captain. You, your friend here,' the Major's automatic waved gently towards Mostyn. 'And his friends as well. All of you.'

'All right. What do you . . .'

'Intend to do?' The Major finished it off with a lift of his eyebrows, then gently shepherded the Captain and Mostyn to the bridge windows. The officer of the watch, helmsman and signaller remained still, held down by the other weapons.

'We are going to do a straight switch.' The Major like a small boy showing off his toy. 'A straight switch of crews. The new crew is on board now. Those Marines down there, they are the new crew. Now the old crew has got to be persuaded to climb down those scrambling nets into the cutter. You think they'll do that?'

'They haven't got much option, have they?' said Mostyn.

'No, chum, they haven't. You come from Boston or swinging London?'

'I'm British,' said Mostyn, all Union Jacks and old Empire.

'Jollee good, what?' mimicked Gladzinsky.

'After your crew has gone down into the cutter, you follow,' continued the Major.

'You'll not get far . . .' began Bone.

'On the contrary. *You'll* not get far.' The Major chuckled. 'There's only enough fuel on board that cutter to take you about twenty miles. And there's no radio. I don't have to remind *you*, Captain, that you've been sailing your boat way off the shipping lanes so you're lost, man.'

'We'll manage.' Bone gave him a cold-as-yesterday's-Baked-Alaska stare. 'And I still don't think you're going to get far.'

'I don't intend to.' The Major looked smug. 'You see I'm only in charge of this part of the operation. We've got a new captain and our commander on board. When I get off, I go with the cutter that's going to play at being you for a few days. You have been sailing under radio silence haven't you? Except for the two quick broadcasts each day so that security knows you're okay?'

Bone perceptibly wilted. 'If you say so.'

'I say so. Twice daily, at midnight and noon, you

77

repeat the words Whisky Zebra ten times on a frequency of . . . but I don't have to tell you, Captain. Anyway, you won't have to worry about that any more, will you? We'll keep on your course for a while so nobody will know what's happened to the *Warbash Admiral* and her cargo until it is too late.' He paused, then added as an after-thought. 'By the way, the cutter has plenty of provisions. You won't starve. But it will be a week or so before they pick you up. Now, will you tell all your sailor boys what to do?'

'Go to hell,' spat the fat Bone.

'Have it your way, chum.' The Major hunched his shoulders and nodded to Gladzinsky who crossed to the bridge microphone, switched on to the loudspeaker system and spoke in a nasal, flat, unemotional drone.

'Hear this, hear this. All crew members and passengers will disembark from the *Warbash Admiral* using the scrambling nets provided on the port side. You will do this under the supervision of the Marine detachment. Men lined up on the port side will disembark first. Now note this. Anyone not complying with this order, or the instructions of the Marines nearest to them, will be shot.' Gladzinsky treated the bridge to another of his smiles as he switched off the speaker system. 'I mean that as well,' he said.

'I don't doubt it,' Bone replied acidly. Then, turning to the Major. 'What do you expect to get out of this?'

'Don't ask me, Captain, I'm just a mercenary. I get paid for doing what I'm told. Now you'll have to excuse me while I just see how we're getting on with your crew.'

'Stalemate?' The Captain queried, raising his eye-brow and looking at Mostyn once the Major had left the bridge.

'Looks like it,' replied Mostyn. 'Got us hard by the short and curlies. I wouldn't try arguing with all this stuff around.' He indicated the assorted weapons confronting them. 'Leave it.'

'Not so worried about them. It's the board of inquiry that bugs me.'

'You and me both,' said Mostyn.

Half an hour later Mostyn was climbing down the scrambling net on to the large ocean-going cutter below.

The crew of the *Warbash Admiral* were now all transferred. With the resignation and defeat which is only felt by men forced to do something against their will at gun point, they had quickly set about finding themselves quarters in the cramped space of the cutter.

Griffin and Chicory stood near the rails as Mostyn landed on deck. Chicory had an arm on his sleeve, her eyes wide with anxiety. 'Boysie?' she asked, 'Isn't Boysie with you?'

'No,' said Mostyn quietly, a glint of hope in his manner. 'I thought he was with you.'

Captain Bone was now on deck. They were hauling up the nets and casting off.

'Where is he?' Chicory had the makings of possible hysteria. 'Where's Boysie?'

'He hasn't come off?' Mostyn looked at Griffin.

Griffin shook his head. 'Not 'ere.'

'Well do something about it. We can't leave him . . .'

'Leave who?' Frankenstein joined them.

'Boysie, Boysie hasn't come off the *Warbash Admiral* . . .'

'Shut up,' said Mostyn with some authority.

'But . . .'

'We leave Boysie where he is.' Mostyn smiled for the first time since they had been boarded. 'We leave him just where he is, because with him on board I'm the only person who can lead us to the *Warbash Admiral* and her *Saturn* rocket.'

'With Boysie on board you can . . .'

'Yes. If they keep him alive that is,' Mostyn added as an afterthought.

'I think we'd best take a trip up to see the Captain.' The Marine prodded Boysie with his carbine.

'Ah,' said Boysie trying to assess the situation. 'That would be Captain Bone? The fat one?'

The Marine shook his head.

'Not Captain Bone?' tried Boysie. 'I see. I am on the *Warbash Admiral*?'

'You're on the *Warbash Admiral* but Cap'n Bone don't live here no more.' The Marine prodded Boysie again. He began to move, slowly. Inside the superstructure there seemed to be more crew members than he had previously seen. And they were all dressed in Marine uniform. Boysie decided that it must be a dream. He would wake up soon, maybe by the time they reached the Captain's cabin.

By the time they got to the Captain's door Boysie had given up the idea that he was dreaming. The Marine tapped on the wood and opened up, pushing Boysie in front of him.

'Seems we missed one,' he said by way of explanation.

'So what have we here?' A tall man stood in the centre of the cabin. Tall and big with a leathery face and cold eyes.

'Move out of the way, Solomon. Let, how do you say it, the dog see the rabbit.' The voice was husky with a slight Latin accent. The big man called Solomon moved and the voice's owner was revealed sitting behind the Captain's desk.

Dressed in a striped jersey, the girl pushed her yachting cap on to the back of her short jet hair. The view, from Boysie's position, was exceptionally delightful. She was a sinewy beauty with an olive complexion and fine dark features. The eyes, into which Boysie looked with some ardour, were a heavy brown and her lips parted in a smile which showed off a set of toothpaste-commercial teeth.

'My, my, my,' she said. 'Are you my first real live stowaway?'

'You're not Captain Bone,' said Boysie playing it dumb.

'No, darling.' She rose displaying a snake-like figure. 'No, I'm not Captain Bone. I'm the new captain.'

'Good. I like you better'n Captain Bone.' Boysie grinned.

'I think you're cute as well.' The girl came round to the front of the desk. She was wearing bell-bottom navy pants below the striped jersey.

'I don't wish to sound inquisitive,' said Boysie trying to be pleasant, 'But I haven't seen you on board before. Or you.' He added looking at the big man.

'No, you wouldn't have.' The man looked at him, a schoolmaster glaring at an obnoxious pupil. 'We didn't come on board until this morning.' He turned to the Marine. 'You'd better wait outside.'

The Marine nodded and left, closing the cabin door behind him.

'I can't understand,' continued the big man, 'how we came to miss you.'

'Miss me?'

'Yes. We cleared the ship. I thought everybody had been taken off.'

Dawn began to break in Boysie's mind. Out of the half-light he spoke. 'You mean that Captain Bone and his merry men are no longer with us. What did you do? Make 'em walk the plank?'

The man smiled. 'Something like that.'

'Everyone?' asked Boysie, a beautiful picture of Mostyn teetering on the edge of a plank, being goaded by jeering sailors, filled his mind.

'You should be with them, really.' The girl moved closer to him. He could smell her, a mixture of sun, sea water and a hint of something or other by Estee Lauder.

'Don't provoke him, Constanza.' The man spoke softly. Threat hovered between them.

'Oh, don't be such a spoil sport. And I'm not provoking him.'

'What have you really done to Captain Bone and his crew?' asked Boysie. The cabin was getting warm.

'Captain Bone, his crew and passengers have all been put in a large ocean-going cutter, with no radio or compass, plenty of food but very little fuel. They'll be picked up. In a week or so.'

'I wasn't very well this morning.' Boysie patted his stomach. 'In the bathroom for a long time.'

'That's probably how we came to miss you,' said the girl. 'By the way this gentleman is Solomon, he's in charge of security . . .'

'Needs to be with all those wives,' said Boysie before he could stop himself.

'And I am the new captain,' continued the girl. 'My name's Constanza Challis.'

'Can I ask where we're going?'

Solomon laughed. 'Yes. Yes, you can ask. We're off to Wizard.'

'Wizard,' repeated Boysie.

'We're off to see the Wizard the Wonderful Wizard of Oz,' chanted Miss Challis. 'Now we've told you so much you must tell us who you are.'

'Ah . . .' began Boysie, but another voice cut in from the doorway before he could continue.

'His name is Oakes and he specializes in Aerospace Flight Simulators. It may be good to have you on board, Mr. Oakes; we shall see. In the meantime it is nice to meet you again.'

They all turned towards the door. The short, blond bespectacled figure of Doctor Ellerman von Humperdinck stood in the doorway.

CHAPTER FIVE

SORCERER

The silken sorcerer
Who, with his mystic numbers
Doth the universe control:
Earth, stars, constellations,
The very depths of space.

THE MAGICIAN: John Edmunds

'IT's all right, Solomon, Mr. Oakes and I met in the very respectable society of Cape Kennedy.' Von Humperdinck advanced into the cabin, closing the door. 'You have been very free with information.'

'We've not told him anything he'd understand.' Constanza Challis had moved back behind the desk.

'Maybe.' Von Humperdinck's eyes seemed even larger behind the heavy glasses. 'Maybe. What have they told you, Mr. Oakes? That we are bound for a place called Wizard? Good. I will add to that. You see, Wizard is an island, and on Wizard I am known as the Sorcerer.' He chuckled, the wheezy chuckle of an old woman. 'I cannot tell if you are for us or against us . . .'

'I don't even know what you're up to . . .' began Boysie.

'Wait, gently.' Doctor von Humperdinck made quieting gestures with his hands. 'All in good time, Mr. Oakes. All in good time I will tell you what we are to do, then you can make the choice. Help us or don't help us.'

'What happens if I don't want to help you?'

'Oh, we keep you locked up for a few days. When it is all over we set you free. We don't favour violence, do we, Solomon?'

Solomon's expression did not change. 'Only in exceptional cases.' For the first time Boysie noticed that Solomon spoke almost without moving his lips like a bad ventriloquist. Not a man to be trusted. 'Are you sure this is wise?' Solomon asked looking firmly at von Humperdinck.

The little doctor locked eyes with him. 'I am a man of peace, Solomon. I've seen too much blood-letting for one lifetime. But I have ideals. That's why I am here. When Mr. Oakes sees the project and hears the whole story he might well feel drawn to it. We can always do with another specialist.' Von Humperdinck turned to Boysie. 'The only problem,' he said, 'is what to do with you until we get to Wizard.'

'Perhaps I can help.' Constanza Challis moved voluptuously in her seat.

'So?' queried von Humperdinck.

'Well,' she traced a line down her cheek with the forefinger of her left hand. 'We have committed an act of piracy. Right?'

'Ach. Technically, yes I suppose so,' admitted von Humperdinck grudgingly.

'And I am now captain of this ship?'

'That's why we hired you,' Solomon slipped in.

'Ach, yes.' von Humperdinck turned to Boysie. 'Constanza is a clever girl. She is Cuban but has her Master's ticket. Great, no?'

'Great, yes.' Boysie felt the old longings stirring. The situation was farcical. One bloody great space rocket stolen at sea by a female Cuban ship's captain, a German-American space scientist and an English heavy. It was too much. Boysie had reached the point where he really wanted out. Or, if not out, at least a retreat into the womb. Any womb. Constanza may have been a tough ship's master but she was certainly a woman, and you didn't have to stretch your imagination.

84

'I'm trying to make a point.' The seafaring Miss Challis looked hurt.

'Go ahead. Nobody is stopping you,' von Humperdinck gushed.

'I figure that if we have carried out an act of piracy and I am the captain of this ship then I'm a pirate captain.'

'Well? Big deal.'

'In all the old movies we used to see in the States,' continued Constanza, 'pirate captains usually ended up with a captured female. You know Errol Flynn stuff.' She struck a pose standing by the desk. 'And what of me? Am I to be food for sharks?' She sat and twirled imaginary moustaches. 'Ha-ha, me lady, no, you are for finer sport. Take her, men, to me night cabin, and deck her with some of those rich garments we took from the Spanish frigate.' On her feet the imprisoned lady again. 'No, I will not tolerate this behaviour. In sooth I certainly will not be made a lackey for a sea-pillaging rat like you.'

'Solomon,' said von Humperdinck with creased brow, 'what is Miss Challis doink?'

'I'm telling you that I want to take the prisoner, Mr. Oakes here, into my personal custody.'

'Ach, so. What a good idea, Constanza. Excellent,' beamed von Humperdinck.

'Nobody's asked me what I think.' Boysie felt the dialogue had not really been running in his favour. Even in a situation like this he liked to be the centre of attraction.

'Oh, you wouldn't turn down an offer like me would you, Mr. Oakes?' Constanza had come alongside. Boysie cast a leering eye over her superstructure and swallowed. ' 'Course I wouldn't,' he said. 'Only, I liked to be asked.'

'Thank God for that,' muttered Constanza. 'It gets me out of a fix. Most of the officers are queer and they tell me it's bad for discipline if I consort with the crew. This way everybody gets to be happy. Anyway, I fancied you the minute you came in.'

'Glad to be of service.' Boysie felt a quiver of anticipation.

'Good,' Constanza said loudly. 'All right. Take him to my night cabin and deck him out in the fine clothes we took from the Spanish frigate . . .'

'And put a couple of armed guards on the door,' interpolated Solomon. 'Come on, Oakes. This way out.'

'Yes, and I will want to talk with you later also,' said von Humperdinck. 'I think we will all be very good friends, yes. Handle him carefully, Solomon. Carefully.'

'Like eggs.' Solomon spoke without humour.

'See you soon,' crooned Constanza, and with that, Boysie felt Solomon's outsize hand grip hard on his biceps and propel him from the cabin.

Goldberg, Frankenstein and Meyer looked gloomily at Mostyn who was happily holding forth with some authority. The engines had spluttered to a standstill after only a few miles. Now the cutter drifted, in not unpleasant weather, a prey to the currents and winds.

'You see,' Mostyn was saying, 'I have often had reason to mistrust our friend, Oakes. So, when he came into my firm as a co-director, I naturally needed to take some precautions. Happily Mr. Oakes' shoe maker was bribable.'

'His shoe maker?' said the non-comprehending Goldberg.

'His shoe maker.' Mostyn smiled his wise, all-knowing smile. 'Every pair of shoes worn by Mr. Oakes is bugged. The 'Footpad' homing transmitter (Personal) Mark Six. Know it?'

'Sure.' Frankenstein leaned back and hooked his right thumb under his armpit. 'That's the one they issued to some of the Treasury boys isn't it?'

'That's it. Particularly useful because one can pick up its signals from altitude.'

'So all we got to do when we've got out of this mess is send up a few thousand search aircraft.' Meyer was turning sarcastic.

'Hardly,' replied Mostyn, still omnipotent. 'I believe certain calculations can be made by the *Warbash Admiral*'s navigation officer. The area of search will be narrowed down.'

'We've got to get ourselves rescued first.' Frankenstein looked at Mostyn as though it was all his fault.

'And what do you think I ought to do about that, chummy,' drawled Mostyn. 'Hang me knickers from the yard arm or something?'

Night at sea. The gentle sensual throb of engines and the arrow-head of foam cutting away from the ship's bows. Water, deep as a trance, rocking them far above the cradle of the deep. Only the horizon visible. Black sea running to the edge of the world and giving way to the heavy pearl of a night sky. Two shades separated by a slim line which ran full circle in the distance.

Constanza came to her night cabin around seven-thirty, excused herself immediately and made for the bathroom. Just after eight she emerged and Boysie's heart quickened. She had changed from jersey and pants into a sleek, hugging black number which made her look exclusively feminine.

'Evenin', Cap'n.' Boysie tugged at his forelock. His clothes had been brought up to the Captain's night cabin on Constanza's orders, and Boysie who rarely looked the proverbial gift horse in the larynx, had taken pains with his appearance: midnight blue slacks and the white silk roll-necked shirt with wide sleeves, his chin carefully barbered, and practically every *Aramis* preparation put to good use.

After dressing, Boysie had stretched himself out on the wide, comfortable bunk, allowed his eyes to wander round the austere cabin. A framed photograph of a large lady grinning, her beefy arms encircling a pair of fat children provided the only relief. Mrs. Bone and the little Bones, thought Boysie.

After an hour or so a couple of the Marines came in and dumped three suitcases. Boysie began to muse over the situation. Never one for running after trouble, he had the wit to see that, however pleasantly his captors treated him, he was dealing with people obviously intent on causing some major globe-shaking shock.

As he saw it, his duty lay in doing the maximum amount of damage with the minimum amount of personal risk. Constanza Challis may well be the most off-beat sea captain he was ever likely to meet, but she certainly offered him an advantage in that he ought to find out something from her during the softer moments of what promised to be a sultry relationship.

Two blond, and unreservedly camp, young stewards served dinner to Boysie and Miss Challis, a reasonable meal of pea soup, which the stewards referred to as *potage Longchamps,* followed by lamb garnished with rosemary, the whole rounded off with *crêpes citron.*

Over dinner they sketched in their personal backgrounds. Boysie giving Constanza a colourful fictitious story of public school and Cambridge followed by a fantastic life in space research. He even hinted at courageous acts performed during World War Two, leaving her with the distinct impression in reality he was an English milord who only worked because he enjoyed it.

Constanza gave a more guarded picture of her life in Havana, both before and after Castro. Her father, she said, had been one of the wealthiest ship owners in Cuba. Strict with his four children, he made each one prepare for the hard realities of life by learning a trade. As a child

Constanza had spent all her spare time around the ships.

'I had the ocean in my blood and I was what you call a tom cat,' she said.

'Tom boy,' corrected Boysie. Constanza simply shrugged.

When Castro took over, her father's ships, together with most of his fortune, became part of the state's assets. But for Constanza it made little difference. She took her Master's Ticket and, for a year, was the only woman captain in Castro's fleet. Eventually, fed up with taking orders, she had run for America, a country which she found so completely decadent she decided to live simply for kicks, helping out those most allied with Castro's ideals for preference.

Eventually the two stewards left them alone with the coffee. Constanza crossed to the door and locked it firmly.

'You're really only an adventuress then?' said Boysie, spilling coffee into their cups.

'You might say that. I don't like taking orders. That's my real trouble.'

'But you'll take orders for money?'

'Doesn't everyone have a price?' The way she said it was as though she had resigned herself to a way of life that she did not really countenance.

'What price the job you're on now?'

'They pay me well.'

'No. I'm sorry.' Boysie struggled to explain. ' "What price" is an English expression. I mean how do you like the job?'

She laughed, showing her fine teeth and the pink tip of her tongue. 'This is a good one. It has everything. Money. Excitement. Danger.'

'There's danger all right.' Boysie looked serious. 'You know you're probably going to get caught?'

'I don't think that's where the danger lies.'

'No? What if Captain Bone and the crew get picked

up sooner than you expect? They're going to have an awful lot of people looking for you.'

'Looking for the *Warbash Admiral* maybe. But the *Warbash Admiral* has disappeared.'

'Disappeared?'

'We have a new name on the side. Now we are sailing in the *Prince of Denmark*.'

'You'll have to change more than the name.'

'We have done that also.'

'You think of everything.' Boysie near to admitting defeat.

'Not me. Those who employ me. Solomon organized most of it. It's wonderful what a few sheets of canvas will do. Even from the air she will look like a merchant ship. Certainly not a tanker.'

'A few sheets of canvas?'

'Stretched over light frames. We've given her a whole new superstructure amidships and changed the line of the bridge. It's quite wonderful I promise you.' Constanza paused, looking at him with predatory hunger, the tiny tip of her tongue darting quickly between her lips. 'Enough talking, my prisoner,' she said, smiling. 'Come.' Constanza stood, stretching out her hand towards Boysie.

'Now wait a minute, baby . . .' began Boysie.

'I am the captain of your ship, Boysie. Come. I don't like to be kept waiting.' The smile had gone. Her hand caught Boysie by the wrist and pulled him, not unwillingly, to the bunk.

'Now look, Constanza . . .' Was all he managed to say before both of her long-fingered hands came up to his shoulders and pushed him back on to the bunk. She fell on him, her lips closing on his like leeches. It was as though the male and female roles were reversed. Boysie even found himself struggling for a second until he relaxed and responded to the gentle probing of her tongue.

The kiss went on for ever, diving down through nine thousand fathoms of lust, Constanza writhing, pushing her body against his so that, in spite of their clothing, they revealed everything to each other. Then her hand slid to his knee and began its slow upward search. His zip came down easily and the hand continued its journey to end wrapped hard around him as her other hand took his and guided it to her breast.

She shifted, beginning to undress him slowly, occasionally slipping her lips from his mouth to bite gently on his ear or whisper soft moans.

His own right hand moved from her breast, feeling its way easily to her knee and upwards as her legs opened wide, his hand finding the damp nylon of her pants between her thighs, warm and velvet to the touch.

Boysie lay naked and ready for her. She slid from him with a whispered, 'Wait, Boysie. Not long,' and deftly unzipped the back of her dress, slipping her arms from the sleeves, allowing the dress to fall around her feet. She stepped away unclasping her bra, cupping her breasts with her hands before she let the thin fabric and lace fall away to reveal perfect orbs, the skin tight, nipples erect.

Constanza came towards Boysie, hands touching the top of her pants, sliding them down and stepping out in one long flowing movement which brought her to the bunk.

She leaped lightly across Boysie, one hand going down between his thighs, gently goading. Then she mounted him, taking the initiative in strength and speed, riding him in a frenzy, covering his face with kisses and holding on to his shoulders, digging the nails deep into the flesh until the moment when both their bodies arched together and they heard the thunder of heartbeats loud in their eardrums.

'You always as domineering as that?' asked Boysie later as they lay together watching the smoke from their cigarettes drift upwards, curling in blue arcs, then disappearing.

'When I've a mind to. You didn't object.'

'No. As long as I can get my own back.'

Constanza chuckled. 'As much as I like you I doubt if you've got the strength.'

Boysie raised himself on one elbow, then relaxed again in an admission of defeat. 'You're surely going to give me at least one chance. How many nights will we have like this?'

'Four, maybe five.' There was a sudden flicker of realization that she had said too much. 'All right, you caught me,' she acknowledged.

'Then you might as well tell me where we're going.'

'Would you believe Paraguay?' She laughed.

'No. Nor Brazil.'

'Good. But I won't tell you. The Sorcerer may, but I must not.'

'Okay.' Boysie paused. 'You said something strange just now.'

'Strange?'

'You said this job had everything. Money. Excitement. Danger.'

'Yes.'

'Then I said there was a danger in you being caught and you replied that you didn't think that was where the danger was.'

'Yes, I remember.' She was lying on her back. He could still see the glistening damp patches on her skin across the top of her breasts where their bodies had rubbed together.

'Where does the danger lie?'

'Boysie,' she sat up and looked at him, a hand half reaching out for his face. 'I cannot tell you where we are going and I only know part of the whole project, but I want to warn you.'

'Go on.'

'I think you will find von Humperdinck a reasonable man, but do not trust Solomon, that one is bad.'

'I could see that much.'

'Yes, but I also believe the men he works for are ruthless. I have merely been hired to do a job. To sail this ship from point A to point B. After that I become useless. The more I see of Solomon, the more I think I may become completely redundant when we arrive.'

'You mean Solomon may . . .?'

'He might kill me. Or have me killed. It depends on his orders, but it's a distinct possibility.'

'I'll watch out for you.' Boysie's stomach gave a nervous hesitation roll as he said it. Constanza touched his hand.

'Thank you, Boysie.' She said, a hint of anxiety in her eyes. 'Thank you, but watch out for yourself. I think these people would get rid of von Humperdinck if he wasn't so important to them.'

That night Boysie dreamed that he was attempting to assemble the giant *Saturn* rocket under von Humperdinck's instructions while Solomon prodded him with a gun. At last he got the thing together and miraculously it was standing up reaching into the clouds. The next moment he was high up climbing the face of the rocket and being chased by Solomon, he tried hard to cling to the smooth surface. Then the inevitable, the hands clutching empty air and the terror of falling.

He woke sweating in the dark cabin with only the thud of the engines and the steady breathing of Constanza to keep him company.

During the three days that followed, Boysie saw Constanza only in the evenings, and during one of those she was called to the bridge twice. Solomon imposed a strict routine. After breakfast Boysie was left to his own devices until noon when he was taken down to his old stamping ground, the boat deck observation platform, for an hour long exercise. Another hour was given to him during the later afternoon. By the second afternoon Boysie could not help noticing that it was getting appreciably colder and the nights were drawing in, or, as he had once heard a well-known wit observe, the days were making like dwarfs.

On the fourth morning, Constanza arrived in the cabin unexpectedly.

'You won't be going down to the boat deck this morning,' she told him. 'The Sorcerer wants to talk with you.' Then, with a hasty glance at the armed Marine standing just outside the door, she whispered. 'Be careful, Boysie. I'll see you tonight.'

Ellerman von Humperdinck arrived just before noon, beaming and motioning the guard to stay well away from the door.

'A humble place but mine own, doctor.' Boysie made an expansive gesture with his hand.

'Ach. Yes, but you must not call me doctor here, friend Oakes.'

'Why not?'

'Here you must call me Sorcerer.'

'Why Sorcerer?'

'Why not? It is the rules. On secret projects there must always be the sense of intrigue. One must have code names. Surely you've read the novels. In books and movies they always have code names so why should it be different in real life?'

'Yes.' Boysie sadly remembered the years he had spent surrounded by intrigue, codes, ciphers and pseudonyms which he could never quite grasp.

'You must be thinking to yourself that I am a bit of a black horse, no?'

'Sheep,' corrected Boysie. 'A black sheep.'

'Sheep, horses, what's the difference? You think I'm one?'

'Well I gathered at Cape Kennedy you had a reputation. People feared you. You kept them on their toes. Security and all that.'

'Good. Good. A smoke screen, Oakes, a curtain of smoke to hide behind. Draw their attention to weakness in security and they will not think of you when you break the rules. This is why it is good that I am known only as Sorcerer. I hope to go back to Cape Kennedy as soon as this project is completed. I'm only on leave you know.'

'I didn't know, but can I ask who you're working for?'

'Myself, of course. I have worked for Nazi Germany, for the Russians, for America. All of them. Now I work for myself. The project itself? I understand it will go to the highest bidder. Russia has provided a great deal of her own free will, and now, here,' he spread his arms wide to indicate the ship and its cargo, 'the United States is providing one of the necessary elements, not quite of its own free will.'

'What is the project? You said that if I . . .'

'All in good time. I can only tell you of part of the experiment. First, we will reach our destination this afternoon. You know where we are?'

'Well we haven't gone into the Med so I reckon we're either off Greenland or Russia.'

'Good. Very good. You get high marks for observation. We are about two hundred miles off the Northern Russian coast. To be exact, in the Kara Sea, and we are heading for a small island which lies one hundred and twenty miles west of the Severnaya Zemlya group. The island has some unpronounceable name beginning with OZ. That is why we call it Wizard.'

'I see,' said Boysie, quite lost. He had only got

Greenland or Russia by a wild guess and remarks made by Constanza. 'And what do we do at Wizard?'

'We carry out an experiment of great interest and value to space exploration. In fact a stride forward in the space race.'

'On a Russian island? Then you can't be working for yourself. You must be doing it for the crimson lads.'

'The ...? I beg your pardon?' von Humperdinck narrowed his eyes behind the huge glasses.

'Forget it,' said Boysie. 'You must be working for the Reds, the Russians.'

'Not necessarily. For three years now I have been working on the problem of Lifting Bodies.'

'Sort of Burke and Hare stuff.' Boysie smiled, cheerfully proud of his little witticism.

Ellerman von Humperdinck looked at him gravely with creased brows. 'They are working on it as well?' he asked.

'They used to. Not any more though.' It was too difficult to explain. The joke was now a corpse.

'So,' continued the doctor. 'Part, and I must stress that it is only a part, of the experiment concerns my revolutionary Lifting Body. It will amaze you.'

'I can't wait.'

'As you know the Lifting Body is a wingless vehicle designed so that the astronaut can control his re-entry into the earth's atmosphere, and, after that, control his landing as with an ordinary aircraft.'

'Yes.' Boysie's interest rose.

'The Americans have been doing experiments for some time. They have done a lot with the Northrop HL-10 research craft and now they have the SV-5D PRIME.'

'Prime?' repeated Boysie.

'Precision Recovery Including Manoeuvring Entry. But I don't have to tell you that. I forgot you are an expert.'

'So do I when I hear people like you talking.'

'Ach. Good.' Von Humperdinck warmed to the flattery. 'The trouble is that the Americans are fools. Everything must be done just so. One cannot take such-and-such a step until a previous set of experiments has been completed. My position can illustrate this. I have had designs for a perfect Lifting Body since 1966 but they say we can't use it until we reach a certain stage in our own experiments. They admit that I have something ready before its time. That is really why I am here.'

'Don't tell me. You've built your own craft on, what's the name of the place – Wizard?'

'In a nutskin.'

'Shell,' said Boysie.

'Quite extraordinary how it happened. Just after my craft, my Lifting Body, I call it "Sext" by the way.'

'Sext?'

'A little humorous play on words. The Americans have PRIME. So . . .'

It was Boysie's turn to be dim about jokes. 'Sorry.' He said looking blank.

'The ancient Catholic Church offices, services, were called Prime, Terse, Sext, Nones and Compline. The Americans have reached Prime but I am two moves ahead of them so I call my Lifting Body "Sext". No?'

'I suppose so.' Boysie tried a light grin. Why do these guys make such heavy weather of it? Always the same with the eggheads, heavy on the laughs.

'Anyway,' there was no stopping von Humperdinck. 'It was just after my craft was first turned down by the Americans. I was visiting Britain for a conference with a number of European space scientists. I unfolded all my grumbles to Professor Sch . . . No I had better not name him. On this project we call him the Seducer.'

'What does he do? Talk people into taking space rides they don't want to take?'

'He will have to tell you, for his experiment is linked to mine. Just as exciting and probably more important. But, as I was saying, I told him of my troubles and it turned out he had a similar problem, an experiment which was before its time and in which he could interest nobody. But he had a proposition for me. Through some wealthy contacts in the City of London, my friend, the Seducer, had managed to get facilities and money to set up and finance a part of his project. The Russian Government provided the island, Wizard, and one very specialized technician.' Von Humperdinck seemed highly amused at this last revelation.

'So the Seducer asked you to come in with him?'

'Quite. There is a whole launch complex and laboratories and workshops on Wizard. Under my directions we have built Sext and its mother capsule which will be used for the Seducer's experiment. The last thing we needed was a rocket large enough to carry the capsule and Sext into orbit. Tentative feelers were put out. America said no. Russia claimed they could not interrupt their programme. So, we had to borrow a rocket.' He cackled, rubbing his hands together.

Boysie turned the matter over. Finally he said. 'How come hard-headed business men have invested in the project?'

'Simple. As soon as the experiment is under way we offer the results to the highest bidder. And, when you hear the Seducer's experiment you will see how important the outcome will be, both to the space race and for the honour of which every country bids the highest.' He chuckled again. 'It is enough to tell you that there will be two astronauts. One Russian and one American.'

'I'll take your word for it.'

'So. You would like to help me in preparing Sext for this operation?'

Boysie had no alternative. 'If you can't beat 'em, join 'em,' he said.

Doctor von Humperdinck proceeded to launch into an incomprehensible scientific analysis of Sext, its aerodynamic-qualities, fuel and electronic systems and controls. Boysie assimilated about one per cent of the description, and when the doctor left, an hour later, his head was reeling.

Around four, Solomon arrived.

'Get a duffle coat on, Oakes. The Captain and the Sorcerer want you on the bridge. Apparently you've agreed to assist the Sorcerer.'

'That's it, Mr. Solomon. Now I'm a kind of Sorcerer's Apprentice.'

Solomon showed no signs of friendliness. 'Just remember it doesn't give you any special privileges.'

'You mean I'm still going to be treated like a prisoner?'

'More or less. Until we've had a chance to check you out. We'll decide what to do with you when the Silversmith arrives.'

'The Silversmith?' screeched Boysie. 'What gives with all these crazy code names. We've already got the Sorcerer and the Seducer, now we have the Silversmith. Who else is left. You only need the Shafter, the Shagger and Shitter and you've got a round half-dozen.'

'We don't laugh about the Silversmith,' said Solomon without a flicker. 'He's the money man.'

'Well I'm glad you choose the letter S and not F,' grinned Boysie. 'A straight flush in Fs would've really had you in trouble.'

'They're waiting for you.' Solomon stood, lack-humoured, by the door.

As he stepped on to the bridge a sight of extreme beauty met Boysie's eyes. The water ahead of them shone, polished dark glass without a ripple. Though it was late in the afternoon the sky was bathed in a white light, reflecting blues and greys, colours elusive to any artist, from the few scattered clouds. Out on the horizon a long hazed and fragmented lump rose from the sea like some hillock suddenly revealed on the landscape of a flat, forgotten planet.

Ellerman von Humperdinck, the Sorcerer, turned from his place beside Constanza, with a welcoming smile. 'Ah, Oakes. Come and look here.' He pointed towards the horizon. 'There it is. There is the island of Wizard.'

Constanza looked up. 'Nearly at journey's end.' A liquid sadness in her eyes.

'You know what they say,' Boysie touched her arm. 'Journey's end in lovers' meeting.'

Constanza gave him a half smile. March sunshine. Then her face went solemn as she returned to her duties as captain.

Slowly, the lump rose and took on definite shape. A substantial land mass, roughly ten miles long, Boysie reckoned. The snow and ice had not yet completely gone. Inshore they had to slice through thin wedges of ice. The island gave the impression of being fairly flat except for the blackish rocks which climbed upwards menacingly, from the shore. Occasionally these gave way to more gently sloping rises, pitted with areas of snow, between which the rough tundra showed dark.

'It covers an area of around fifty square miles.' The Sorcerer acted as guide. 'There is a bay on the south side which, I understand, they have dredged and converted into a harbour for us.'

'Will it hide the ship from the air?' asked Boysie watching von Humperdinck out of the corner of his eyes.

'We won't have that trouble.' The Sorcerer kept his gaze on the island. 'Weather planes go over once in a while.' Then, looking up with a broad smile. 'But, with any luck the ship will not worry us. We should be able to unload during the hours of darkness and then ...'

'Then what?'

'Then the ship can go.'

'Where? They'll be mounting a full scale search soon. It can't be long anyway.'

'You are probably right. So the ship must go downwards. It must be skittled ...'

'Scuttled.'

'To the bottom. Davy Jones' lock-up.'

'Locker.'

'What you said.'

'And what about Constanza?'

'Solomon is taking care of that. He says she should stay here.'

Boysie felt a twinge of concern. Doctor von Humperdinck was a shade too flip about Constanza's future.

Boysie's thought processes could never be described as Mach Two, but he now had the first stirrings of fear about the ludicrous little doctor. Who the hell do I trust, he asked himself. Certainly not Solomon, he had no soulfeeling about that man. Yet, he had thought of von Humperdinck as merely an eccentric involved with strange outlandish criminal endeavours.

Constanza had acted as a kind of sexual soporific; something to keep his mind in obsession during the journey. Now, he began to wonder how much of that was an arranged and carefully plotted act. Boysie swallowed nervously as they rounded the headland. He could see the entrance to the bay ahead. Perhaps stepping on to the island of Wizard would be his last act. Or worse. You could never tell with those who had a scientific turn of mind. They might well be using him as a guinea pig.

Darkness came rapidly as they entered the bay, which must have been nearly two miles across. Slowly, and with a minimum amount of noise, the *Warbash Admiral* came to rest alongside a thrusting concrete dock which stretched from the harsh-looking shore into the deep central water of the bay. Arc lights flared on from dock and ship, while, before Solomon reappeared on the bridge to take him below, Boysie watched a pair of floating cranes being towed into position, one on the far side of the dock, the other beside the ship. They stood, diametrically opposite one another, as though poised, ready to lock jibs in battle.

In the cabin, Boysie heard the gentle whine of hydraulic jacks opening up the ship's hold and, as the hours passed, he could feel the throb of activity throughout the ship.

Just before nine, Constanza came into the cabin. She looked white and tired.

'Trouble?' asked Boysie, stomach now well aflutter with crazy butterflies.

Constanza put her hand to her mouth, motioning silence until she had closed the door.

'I've been ordered off,' she said, confidence drained from her voice and manner. 'They'll still take an hour or so to finish unloading. But I have to pack. So do you, Boysie. The Sorcerer's friend, the Seducer, is here. He wants to see you.'

'And what about you?' Boysie played it cagey.

'I don't think he'll want me.' Either she was acting with the ability of Peggy Ashcroft or she had already given up. 'Solomon says I will be kept on the island until the Silversmith arrives. His plane will take off – after he's paid me.' She lifted her arms and dropped them again with a sigh. The gesture of defeat. 'Boysie. I don't know what to believe.'

'Politically or . . .?'

'About the whole of this.'

'Nothing much you can do about it now. Anyway I don't suppose they'll be able to keep us very far apart. Shouldn't think they've got the facilities. Living accommodation.'

'You'd be surprised. I gather it's pretty well organized. I just get a bad feeling. I've had it since . . . well, since us . . .'

Boysie, for all the butterflies which seemed to have begun copulating in his guts, decided to pass off the girl's fears.

'Don't worry about me, Constanza,' he said. 'Me, I really ought to have the old tattoo right across my chest. You know, the one that says "find them, phone them, do the other thing and forget them".'

Constanza did not laugh. Boysie noticed his hand was trembling in harmony with the butterflies. 'The worst they can do is kill us.' As he said it, Boysie felt horribly sick. Bloody Mostyn and his American trips, he muttered to himself as he gloomily set about packing. God knows what they thought he was. They were setting him up for something. He was certain about that. But who was conning him to do what? That, as they say, was something else.

Solomon arrived an hour later with four members of his goon squad to help with the baggage.

Two gangways had been let out from the lower bridge deck. Boysie turned his eyes away from the sudden glare of the arc lights as Solomon shepherded them to the top of the forward gangway. The cranes had their metallic noses dipped, like a pair of great rooting birds, into the trough of the *Warbash Admiral's* hold, their chains dangling into the ship's interior.

'Straight down on to the dockside.' Solomon had begun speaking to them as though he held a gun. It was freezing cold and Boysie felt most unhappy. He had taken one step on to the gangway when the loudspeaker system became suddenly active. 'Stop working and stand still everyone.' The disembodied voice echoed uncannily around the bay.

'Kill the arcs.'

The arc lights died, leaving blisters of colour un-
pleasantly bright in the darkness behind the eyes.

'There is an aircraft passing approximately ten miles
east of us,' the voice continued. 'Just keep still until we
know it's gone over.'

Ten miles east of Wizard, the Grumman Albatross
bearing markings of the Luftvorsvaret, the Royal Norwegian Air Force, grumbled its way through the night
sky. Its antennae clawed at the air, trying to catch signals,
while the electronic equipment of the twin-engined search
and recovery aircraft pricked up its ears in the bulbous
radome.

On the flight deck, the radar and electronics officer
suddenly stiffened, turned and shouted in Norwegian,
towards the captain.

'I've got a fix.'

'Can you mark it by yourself? Or do we need another
aircraft?'

'Let me have a go.' The radar and electronics officer
turned back to the controls of his D/F set and the noises
in his earphones.

One signal was weak but predominant. 'Tweet-twit-
twit, twit. Tweet-tweet-tweet. Tweet-twit-twit-twit-twit.
Tweet-tweet-tweet. Tweet-twit-twit-twit. Tweet-tweet-
tweet.' Went the signal, which, being translated, means
'B-O-B-O-B-O'.

CHAPTER SIX

SEDUCER

Thou strong seducer, opportunity!
THE CONQUEST OF GRANADA: John Dryden

IT was not by accident that the flight path of the Norwegian Air Force Gumman Albatross took it only ten miles from Wizard. Its presence was directly attributable to Mostyn.

The ocean-going cutter, in which the *Warbash Admiral*'s crew and passengers drifted had been sighted after only twenty-four hours, by a Portuguese, NATO-committed, Lockheed Neptune.

The aircraft's captain reported the facts to his base: a large cutter adrift with members of the crew waving distress signals. From then on, the cutter was kept under constant air surveillance until the advent of a Portuguese frigate squadron to take them in tow.

After a hurried exchange of signals the squadron commander radioed an alert to all local NATO bases and proceeded to board the cutter. There followed a long and heated conference which resulted in Mostyn being lifted out by helicopter, the commander realizing that Mostyn was the most important link between any NATO forces and the missing *Saturn V*. By this time frantic messages were pulsing out and the strategic brains of NATO were becoming edgy, the purloining of a multi-million US space rocket being not the happiest way to keep the balance of power.

By lunchtime on the third day, Mostyn arrived, somewhat awestruck, at ACE, Allied Command Central Europe. There the Generals, Admirals and Air Marshals, pink, puffed and purple, listened attentively to Mostyn's evidence concerning the jolly-rogered trip on the *Warbash Admiral* and resultant theft of the rocket. Not unnaturally they showed special interest on hearing of Mostyn's Search Homer lodged in Boysie's shoes.

By evening, NATO search and recovery aircraft were taking off for the needle-in-the-haystack survey over the thousands of miles which made up a possible area in which the relatively small *Warbash Admiral* might be lurking.

A night and a day passed. Mostyn, incarcerated at ACE, began to smell defeat. Then, late on the fourth evening since the boarding of the *Warbash Admiral*, he was hurried to the Deputy Supreme Allied Commander Europe.

The Deputy SACEUR was a young Brigadier, a fact which vaguely niggled Mostyn who had spluttered out, rank-wise, on reaching Colonel.

'Come in and sit down, Colonel Mostyn.'

Mostyn sat, upright, at attention, eyeing the red tabs with basic jealousy.

'Smoke?' The Brigadier stood up, pushing the cigarette box across the desk.

Mostyn nodded acceptance. He was beginning to feel a shade uneasy. The Brigadier vaguely reminded him of his old chief at Special Security, with whom interviews usually led to danger, or, more often, disaster.

'Yes.' The Brigadier sucked his teeth as Mostyn lit a cigarette and blew a thin stream of smoke ceilingwards. 'Yes, Colonel.' Reflectively. Then: 'You had an interesting career in Intelligence. Envy you really. You enjoyed it?'

'It was my life.' Mostyn noncommittal.

'What about this other chap? What's 'is name . . .?'

The Brigadier looked down at a folder lying open on his desk, 'Oakes? What about him?'

'Well what about him, sir?'

'What kind of chap? Obviously didn't trust him a great deal. The homers in his shoes and all that skulduggery, what?'

'Not that I don't trust him . . .' Mostyn started, suddenly realizing this could be a nasty catch question. 'It's . . . well, Boysie has a habit of drawing trouble like a poultice draws a boil. I simply felt happier having him bugged.'

'Ha. Bugged Boysie. Good, eh? What?'

'Ha-ha,' said Mostyn waxing humorous as one always does when a senior officer makes a funny.

'Yes. Decidedly fruity. How would you like to be back in the field, Colonel Mostyn?'

'In what way?' Mostyn asked slowly, as though treading barefoot through a sewer.

'We're a bit stuck to be honest.' The Brigadier pulled at a curtain cord behind his desk. The drapes moved back to display a map: The Arctic Ocean and its environs.

'An Albatross aircraft from the Norwegian base at Spitzbergen,' his finger jabbed at the map, 'has picked up Oakes' homer signals.'

Mostyn was on his feet as though rectally stung. 'Where?' he queried peering at the map.

The Brigadier's finger traced slowly across the cold paper ocean until it came to rest on a tiny spot. It might even have been a fly dropping. 'Here,' he said. 'Your boy is here, one of the outer islands of the Severnaya Zemlya group. Place called Ozshanya. Off the main routes. Uninhabited, but we've had reports of some activity there during the last eighteen months.'

'Russian soil?'

'Yes, but they claim to have rented it out. Private industry. A weather station and experimental area. That's all we know.'

'And that's where Boysie is?'

'That's where at least one pair of his shoes are. Can't rule out the possibility of him being slipped overboard, washed up here, eh?'

'What do you want me to do?'

'Tricky situation really. But we thought you would probably be the best person to do it.'

'Do what?' persisted Mostyn.

'You done any parachuting lately?' asked the Brigadier with a winsome smile.

'Not lately,' replied Mostyn, catching the drift of the situation.

'Pity. Still I expect you'll get used to it. Like swimming really. See here that you were parachute trained and did several operational drops.' He was consulting the folder again.

'That was a long time ago.'

'So you said. But he is your boy, isn't he? I mean it would be best to send you, wouldn't it? You'd be in a better position to evaluate the situation.'

'Boysie can evaluate his own position. If he's alive then the bloody rocket is probably there with him. That's all the evaluation you need.'

'Softly, softly I'm afraid, Colonel. Delicate situation. Still technically Russian soil. But if you happened to drop from the skies, make contact, report that the rocket is there, but no Russians, then we would be able to take action.'

Mostyn made no reply.

'You leave for Spitzbergen tonight.' The Brigadier breezy as a travel agent. 'Once there you'll come under the direct command of C-in-C AFNORTH.'

'AFNORTH?'

'Allied Forces Northern Europe. C-in-C's one of ours.

A general. He's on his way from HQ Kolsaas to Spitzbergen. He'll see you well briefed and kitted out.'

'And what if I refuse?'

'Oh, you can't.' The Brigadier sounded almost offended. 'You can't possibly. You really should read the small print, Colonel. We're quite at liberty to call you up in time of emergency, you and Major Oakes, both.'

'In time of emergency,' stressed Mostyn.

'Didn't I tell you? Forget me head next. As far as NATO is concerned we are on Condition Red until that *Saturn V* is returned. I mean you can't go pinchin' a damn great rocket and expect to get away with it, can you?'

An hour later, Mostyn took off for Spitzbergen.

The darkness and silence went on for a good fifteen minutes. Then the disembodied voice once more echoed round the bay.

'Resume operations. Okay lights, she's gone, nothing to worry about.'

'And down we all go.' Solomon was behind them, breathing, Boysie felt, down the back of his neck. Not that Boysie minded, his limbs being almost frozen by the long, cold wait. The arcs were unleashed again, drowning the scene with their uncompromising light.

At the bottom of the gangway, on the concrete dockside, stood a BV 202 articulated-steering tracked vehicle. That was what it was, though Boysie did not know a BV 202 from a corporation dustcart. To him it simply looked like any other squat, metallic and ugly half-track transporter.

The goons went to the rear section and began to load the baggage. The driver nodded to Solomon and continued to stamp and blow his hands, breath turning into visible clouds as it hit the cold air. At last Boysie and Constanza were ushered into the rear section. Solomon joined them, sitting opposite on the hard bench seats which ran up each side of the interior. The engine, which had been idling, now roared high. Gears thudded and the vehicle moved off up the dockside.

The rear canvas flap had been lowered, so Boysie had no view, nor could he judge either distance or direction. The ride lasted for fifteen minutes or so. At last the BV 202 came to a standstill. The canvas flap was raised and Solomon motioned them to get out. Two men stood by the tail, both dressed in light coloured parkas, hoods up against the cold. They also had rifles slung across their shoulders and, as they turned, Boysie saw that each carried a large white circle stitched to the back of their clothing.

They had stopped in front of a long low complex, single storeyed and stretching around them in an E shape. The air felt even colder than it had done on the bay. Somewhere to the right, a dog howled.

'Straight in,' said Solomon pointing to the glass-doored entrance hall. Inside, a large woman in slacks and white roll-necked jumper waited. Constanza, who had not spoken since they left the cabin, glanced quickly up at Boysie and smiled nervously, as though looking to him for reassurance. Boysie could offer none. To him the large lady looked like a wardress, skilled in massage and other less therapeutic arts. She stepped forward as they approached.

'Captain Challis?' In front of Constanza.

Constanza nodded the affirmative.

'If you would follow me, please, I'll show you to your quarters.' The woman had a gruff, lesbian manner.

Constanza switched her gaze from Boysie to Solomon, the eyes pleading more than questioning.

'Go with her, Constanza. There are only five women here including yourself. Three of those are for female protection, which you just might need.''

Constanza nodded.

'One of the men'll bring your luggage,' said the large lady, taking her by the arm.

She looked back once, and Boysie began to sense the appalling claustrophobic atmosphere of a prison. He looked at Solomon. 'Where's mine?' He asked trying to make his lips smile. Instead of a smile the left side of Boysie's mouth twitched nervously, a sure sign that the screaming terror would soon rack his body and mind.

'You don't get one of those,' replied Solomon. 'You seem to be privileged at the moment. The Sorcerer's waiting for you with the Seducer.'

'What's holding us up then? Let's get this show on the road.'

'Follow me.'

Solomon set off up the passage which led straight on to the entrance hall. The interior of the complex was a cross between a hospital and an office building. Boysie glanced through the glass panels in some of the doors which they passed, the interiors showed neat hygienic rooms, some furnished with beds, some with desks and IBM typewriters. One was filled with rows of chairs facing a blackboard and great maps, another looked like a small well-stocked library. The floors beneath their feet were waxed to a fine polish and the air seemed to be heavy with an antiseptic smell, which Boysie associated with clinics and nursing homes, but could not place.

At last Solomon stopped beside a plain door on which he tapped. A voice told him to enter and they stepped into an office room, decorated and furnished austerely. Three leather chairs and an unpolished desk. Doctor von Humperdinck stood in front of the desk, behind which sat a small rodent-like man. He wore a crumpled worsted suit and his sparse dark hair had a tendency to drop forward in a moth eaten fringe which he constantly had to brush from his eyes.

'Ah,' Humperdinck greeted them. 'Here is the wise Solomon and the Sorcerer's Apprentice.' He smiled, but the man behind the desk showed no emotion.

'Thank you Solomon. You may go for the time being. Mr. Oakes will stay with us here.'

The rodent-like man had a nasty fanatical flash in his eyes that Boysie did not like.

'Sit down, Mr. Oakes,' said Ratty.

'I am sorry, you do not know each other. No.' Humperdinck took a step towards the desk. Boysie heard the door close as Solomon left. 'This is the Seducer. Seducer this is my Apprentice . . .'

'Yes,' said the Seducer, without much love in his voice. 'I know this is Mr. Oakes. But, Mr. Oakes, I do not know much about you. I know you were on board the *Warbash Admiral*. But in what capacity, Mr. Oakes? What capacity?' He had a smooth accent. Originally German, Boysie presumed, with the gutturality removed. He did not take to the Seducer.

'Capacity?' he said trying to act dumb.

'Don't play for time. Just tell me.' This character operated like a movie Gestapo agent. Boysie was suddenly overtaken by a feeling of distinct insecurity.

'Oh. You mean what capacity,' he said, blustering. 'Yes. Well. To be honest I was bumming a trip home. I've been over in the States doing some liaison work. On the new Aerospace Flight Simulator. I'd been advised of the *Saturn*'s shipment to the UK. I just asked for a lift. Simple as that.' Boysie lied, feverishly hoping for the best.

'Then you were not with the technical staff?'

'What technical staff?'

For a moment that seemed to pacify the Seducer. 'Then if you were not with the technical staff, were you by any chance concerned with security?'

'Not guilty,' said Boysie, crossing his fingers to ward off the evil eye.

'He is most interested in the project,' interpolated the Sorcerer.

'You told me,' replied the Seducer. 'You have only told him of your part of the operation?'

'What else? I am only concerned with my part of the experiment, though yours is undoubtedly the more interesting.'

The Seducer tapped his teeth with a pencil, stood up and walked round the desk as though inspecting Boysie. At last, 'He would make an admirable back-up for my experiment.'

'You need a back-up?'

'Why do you think I have kept Miss Challis here? The next three days will be crucial. The slightest cold, a sore throat, some minor disorder and the test could be ruined.' He turned to Boysie. 'You have no sexual deviations?'

'Hey, what do you mean by . . .?'

'I mean you are not queer?'

'I . . .' Boysie half-rose, furious.

'I think you can take the answer as being in the negative,' said the Sorcerer. 'Or you could ask Captain Challis.'

'Yes,' said Boysie, anger having taken over from fear. 'You do that. You ask Constanza. What's sex got to do with it anyway?'

Both the Seducer and the Sorcerer laughed. 'You may have a chance to find out. It could be most pleasant for you. It could also make you. Money and fame I mean.'

A hundred images were floating round Boysie's mind. The words which came from both the Seducer and the Sorcerer were simply words. He could not reach behind the words and find any pattern or meaning. Space. Sexual deviations. Cold. A sore throat. Back-up. Constanza was a back-up. What the hell . . .?

Boysie came out of the strange tangled conversation to

hear the Seducer saying, '... She is being given the tablets now. They will bring her rhythm in line with that of Sonya. This is why we only have three days.' The Seducer wheeled round on Boysie. 'One simple question, Mr. Oakes.'

It'd better be bloody simple, thought Boysie putting on his intelligent face, the one that made him look even more vacant, like a male model.

'Tell me,' began the Seducer, 'what are Kelper's Laws?'

He might as well have asked Boysie to fly round the room or collect droppings from a rocking horse.

'Kelper's Laws?' Boysie playing for time. Five seconds felt like five minutes.

Then chaos broke loose. A clamour of bells, followed by a weird, low, hooting noise.

The Seducer belched a Teutonic oath and dived for the door. High in the passageway Boysie saw a small panel now flashing with red light. A crimson arrow pointing down the passage towards the entrance hall and pulsating in time with the hooting noise. Solomon was already running. Like sheep, the Sorcerer and the Seducer followed, with Boysie puffing slightly in the rear.

They reached the entrance hall, a shaft of freezing air bursting in as Solomon breasted the doors like a runner at the tape. By the time they reached the outside, Solomon was dashing away from, and to the left of, the building. Three spotlights were fingering, pointing to the left, probing as though trying to pin something down. Then, first one shaft of light, then the others, converged on one spot. A small, lone figure, whirled like some grotesque dancer, the arms trying to cover its eyes. Boysie stood fascinated, barely noticing that the Seducer and the Sorcerer were beside him.

Across the freezing night they heard Solomon shouing. 'Stop. Stand quite still. Stop, otherwise ...' The rest of the sentence was carried away by the air and a hungry yelping of dogs.

There were two of them, huge Alsatians, bearing down on the little twisting figure still making a desperate bid for safety. Solomon was shouting again as the first dog leaped and brought the figure down. Then the other dog was in, growling and tearing as the creature screamed, loud, shrill piercing and horrible screams. Shrieks of anguish suddenly merging into one single high-pitched cry which died at its apogee.

Solomon's arm was up. Three flashes from his hand followed by three cracks as the sound of his automatic, fired into the air, reached the little group of watchers by the entrance to the complex.

The dogs turned towards Solomon. They stood still and quivering, occasionally tossing their heads in a low growl towards the bundle which lay motionless at their feet. Another figure had now appeared in the circle of light thrown by the spots. He was calling to the dogs. They obeyed him somewhat reluctantly, moving towards him, away from the bundle.

'I didn't mean it to happen. It was so sudden. I was giving her the tablets when she pushed me to one side and ran for it. I couldn't help it.'

Boysie only part-recognized the voice. Turning he saw the large wardress lady, now shaken and trembling. Then, the implications struck home. 'You bastard,' he shouted, 'God help you.' And he began to run towards the tableau of Solomon, the dog-handler and the still figure on the ground. He heard the Sorcerer shout after him and the sound of feet, but he ran as though the killer dogs were at *his* heels.

Solomon had turned the body over as Boysie reached him. Constanza Challis's face was drawn up in a grim death mask, a face which bore on it the marks of both terror and bewilderment. On the left side of her neck the flesh had been ruthlessly torn, ripped away. Blood had enveloped the ground where the ruptured jugular had spouted out its fountain of dark arterial gore. Boysie turned away and was disgustingly sick into the snow. He swallowed, wiped his eyes and turned. Solomon was on his feet again. Constanza had meant little but an escape into sensuality to Boysie. A ship's captain who had, literally, passed in the night. But his whole sense of affection revolted at this violence. Fists flailing he leapt for Solomon. There was no chance. Fear, panic and anger had combined to unbalance Boysie's judgment. Solomon stepped to one side, lifted his hand and chopped down on to Boysie's neck. The mantle of nauseating blackness and pain closed in.

There was no way of telling how long he had been out. His neck felt bruised and stiff, as though he had been sitting too long in a draught, and there was a whining noise in his ears. Boysie sat upright and shook his head. A wave of sickness passed through him and he could see that his hands were trembling.

He was back in the Seducer's office. Nobody else was there and a strange silence seemed to have enveloped the building. Gingerly, still rubbing the back of his neck, Boysie stood up and walked carefully to the door. Locked. Constanza's dead face swam into his mind. Rage followed close on the vision's heels. Then a terrifying calm. The moment of truth. Anyone who would go to these elaborate safety precautions was a guilty man. Boysie knew he had to stay in this place and find some method of either sabotage or revenge.

He looked round. There was a folder lying open on the desk. Flipping through its pages, Boysie saw easily that it needed a better man than him to make anything out of the graphs and equations laid out black against the snow white paper.

The book shelf. Crammed with erudite tomes. *Rocket Engines. Cosmic Dust.* Wernher von Braun's *Space Frontier.* Boysie did not really know what he was looking for. Then, it almost leaped out. A small book with black and blue lettering on the spine. *Dictionary of Astronautics.* Quickly he riffled through the pages. H-I-J-K, what was it? Knudsen Number; Kappa IV; Capustin Year; Kelvin Scale; no. Here. That was it. Kepler's Laws. Dropping into a chair, Boysie started the painful process of committing three paragraphs to memory.

His head ached, eyes were sore. The seconds whipped by. Minutes. An hour perhaps. All sense of time seemed to have gone. Then the sound of footsteps. Catting it across the room, Boysie returned the book to its place and flopped out in the chair. The door opened. He groaned, sat up and shook his head.

'Ah, so you are awake.' The Sorcerer faced him. Boysie thought the man looked white and shaken. The Seducer, behind him, seemed unmoved.

'You were foolish to attack Solomon,' said the Seducer, 'it shows grave lack of control.'

'A pity you didn't show any . . .' Boysie began.

'You think we are insensitive?' Humperdinck spat out. 'She was a good girl. Talented. Might have done great things.'

'She panicked.' The Seducer looked at the floor. 'I blame Solomon. She should have been warned about the dogs. Once they are let loose . . . You will not make the same mistake, Mr. Oakes.'

Boysie stayed silent.

'Are you ready to finish our conversation?' asked the Seducer.

'Go ahead. Whatever you like.'

'Now I've lost my back-up for Sonya she must be isolated completely. I only hope Mr. Oakes is a fit person to back-up Yetsofar.' The Seducer spoke to the Sorcerer. He turned back to Boysie. 'Ah, yes. One simple question. If you are so clever, Mr. Oakes. What are Kelper's Laws?'

Boysie took a deep breath and plunged with his eyes shut. 'Kelper's Laws. First: Every planet moves in an ellipse having the Sun at one focus. Second: The radius vector sweeps out equal areas in equal times. Third: The squares of the periodic times are proportional to the cubes of the mean distances from the Sun.'

He might just as well have been reciting from the Jerusalem telephone directory, in Hebrew, for all it meant to him. But it seemed to please both the Seducer and the Sorcerer.

'Good,' beamed the Seducer, the first smile Boysie had seen from him. 'I don't wish to seem inhospitable, Mr. Oakes, but as you have already seen tonight, we have to be careful. You are still willing to assist?'

'I'll help the Sorcerer, certainly,' said Boysie. 'But, shouldn't I know something about your side of the experiment?'

'In good time. In good time,' nodded the Seducer. 'Solomon, naturally, does not feel well disposed towards you. He has asked us to keep you informed only of essential things for the time being. The Silversmith arrives tomorrow, and the day after that we will begin the count down. Three days from now you will feel pleased at having taken part in such an operation.'

The Seducer opened the door. 'Come.' He spoke pleasantly to Boysie.

They led him down the passage to another door which opened into a luxurious suite, plush as any three star hotel. Deep pile carpet, sumptuous bed, a bathroom which would not have looked out of place at an international display of cleansing facilities. Piped music, filtered from a speaker housed above the bed. Boysie's case stood by the bed, and a small table had been laid for dinner. A prawn cocktail nestled comfortably in its little goblet, while a side table creaked under its little load of cold chicken, ham, tongue and a vast salad bowl. There was also fresh fruit and cheese, while, in the centre of the table, a silver ice bucket sprouted a bottle of Dom Perignon.

'Eat, bathe and get some sleep,' said the Seducer.

Boysie nodded, crossing to the window and drawing back the curtains. Outside he could just discern the flat black and white landscape, barren and as bleak as the road to Hell. He shivered, turning quickly on hearing the door close. The Seducer and the Sorcerer had left and from the door came, first the click of a key turning, then the strange snuffle and pawing of a dog on guard.

Mostyn landed at Spitzbergen in the early hours. A British major met him and apologized on behalf of the C-in-C AFNORTH. 'He arrived two hours ago,' said the Major, 'He's catching up on his sleep.'

Mostyn nodded grumpily and was taken to the Base Hospital where a pair of tired and disgruntled medics were awaiting him. There followed an exhaustive physical, checking and re-checking, before he was allowed to go with the Major to the Officers' Mess where a meal and bed were ready for him.

'Tomorrow we'll just go through your parachute technique again, sir. Then you'll have to spend a little time with stores before we do a briefing. You go tomorrow so we haven't much time.'

'Can't wait, laddie, can't wait,' said Mostyn tartly.

CHAPTER SEVEN

SEXT

It is the bell for Sext, my lord;
The time for prayer;
In sooth 'tis prayers you need.
THE UNHOLY: John Bracegirdle

BOYSIE'S neck was still stiff when they woke him the following morning. One of the guards, with the white roundel on his back, brought breakfast, English style, bacon and eggs, toast and marmalade and a large pot of coffee.

The same guard returned to remove the dishes and leave a set of clothes.

'Orders are that you put these on,' was his only comment.

Boysie picked up the clothes, garment by garment. A suit of woollen long johns, a pair of heavy calf-length stockings, high boots with tough rubber soles, a thick blue coverall with zipped pockets, a pair of fleece-lined gloves and a light coloured parka. On the back of the parka a white circle had been stitched.

Slowly he climbed into the clothes. He rather liked the effect when he got to the coverall stage, it made him look like a military jet pilot.

'Now hear this. Now hear this,' he growled, watching himself in the mirror. 'Pilots man your planes. Pilots man your planes.' He ran round the room, puffing heavily, then, dragging a chair in front of the mirror, Boysie climbed into it from the side and went about buckling his imaginary safety harness.

'Oscar Tango One. Permission to start engines.' His hand was cupped to his mouth. Then, holding his nose, 'Control to Oscar Tango One. You are clear to start engines.' Pressing the imaginary starter button, Boysie revved the great jets.

'Oscar Tango One. Clear take-off please. Control to Oscar Tango One, you are clear to take-off under supervision of the Catapult Launch Officer.' Boysie looked out of his cockpit, watching the little figure whirling his hand round as Boysie opened the throttle. Maximum revs, then the Catapult Launch Officer dramatically pointed forward and he felt the kick in his back as the jet roared off the flight deck. Climbing now. Gear up. There was a tap at the door and Boysie had to eject back into reality.

The Sorcerer stood in the entrance, face wreathed in smiles. 'Good morning, Apprentice. Hope you feel rested. Now we must go to work.'

Boysie shrugged his way into the parka, zipped it up, picked up his gloves and followed the Sorcerer.

'First,' said the Sorcerer, 'I must introduce you to Sext.'

Boysie nodded. Today was not a talking day. Today was listening and observing day.

They made their way to the main entrance hall. A lightweight G/S Landrover waited outside, the driver was looking impatient. They sky was clear, a light blue, but the cold still ripped into one's body, despite a shining sun.

'Where to, sir?' asked the driver as they climbed aboard.

'Capsule workshops,' ordered the Sorcerer.

The Landrover moved off.

'How many men have we got here?' Boysie felt the odd probing question could do no harm. He had carefully accented the 'we'.

'About two hundred and twenty,' the Sorcerer said blandly. 'One hundred and twenty technicians and launch complex staff. About one hundred guards and HQ personnel.'

'Quite a large operation then.'

'You'll see. You'll see just how big it is.'

The Landrover was following a cinder-based track over the flat landscape. Now they seemed to be turning south. Ten minutes later Boysie caught sight of what looked like a low scaffolded building to their left. The Landrover turned towards the scaffolding which grew as they approached. Slowly Boysie made out the lines of a rocket gantry. It rose higher and higher over the skyline as they approached. Soon they were in the midst of a full-scale launch complex, complete with pad, launch control bunker, and two giant radar aerials, bowls rotating steadily.

Boysie, fascinated, could clearly see that already the first stage of the stolen *Saturn V* was in position at the gantry, while cranes were lifting the second stage into place.

'You could be back at Kennedy, eh?' The Sorcerer was very pleased.

'I wish we were. It's too bloody cold here.'

'The extremes of temperature never really make any difference to me. It is as though I do not notice.'

'Glad you don't. You're lucky, it's killing the brass monkeys.'

'The brass monkeys?'

'Forget it,' said Boysie feeling a shade uppish.

They had come to rest beside a low hangar-like building.

'Here is where the brains hang out,' said the Sorcerer, chuckling.

The building was well guarded. At least four men with rifles stamped their way up and down. There was no military precision about them, but, even in their stamping and slapping shoulders against the cold they gave the appearance of alertness. The Sorcerer led Boysie through a small passage which served as a technicians' entrance. Through a door at the end of the passage and they were in a large hangar. A hangar large enough to have housed Blenheim Palace – twice. In the centre of the big concrete floor stood a space capsule, a great white bulb slightly larger than the Apollo nodule and with a much thicker and longer neck sprouting from its top. To Boysie, the craft looked obscene, like an outsize model womb. Along the side of the capsule black lettering spelled out the legend SKYCHILD ONE.

'She is a beautiful baby, yes?'

'Terrifying,' said Boysie looking up at the spacecraft about which men swarmed. 'This is the one?'

'This is it.'

'Ah. Umm. What about the lifting body?'

'I thought you'd never ask. Come, I show you.'

Boysie followed the Sorcerer across the concrete and into a wide offshoot hangar. The walls were plastered with drawings and maintenance plans. A round table in the centre of the floor held a large model of the space-craft in the other hangar, while to the right stood a squat wooden aircraft with a flat rocket-shaped body, and two long curved rudders and stabilizers. A pair of minute delta-shaped wings protruded from the fuselage, giving the impression that they were apologizing for being there at all.

The Sorcerer followed Boysie's gaze. 'Yes,' he said. 'That is the mock-up of Sext. But later for that, let me show you how things will operate.'

They crossed to the table with its model of *Skychild One*. The Sorcerer removed the outer casing disclosing an interior sectional model. Boysie could now see the reason for the long thick neck of the spaceship. Inside the neck, up-ended and with undercarriage retracted, sat Sext.

'Now you see,' said the Sorcerer. 'My Sext is held in

position here, in the neck of the capsule. You will note that it is completely sealed off by a separate heat shield which will eventually take the impact from Sext's rocket motor. Now,' he pointed. 'You will see each side of Sext is fitted with an aluminium ladder reaching down to traps in the Sext heat shield. Two crew members begin the launch seated in Sext. Once they reach second stage they make their way down ladders and through the heat shield into the capsule. There they will conduct the Seducer's experiment. If there is a fault during launching Sext will automatically be triggered off, the rocket motor shooting it a distance of five thousand feet before the two jets become ignited and the pilot astronaut can take control, stabilize the craft and bring her back to earth like a normal aircraft.' He paused to let the information sink in. 'You follow?'

'Yes. But what about this experiment in the capsule?'

'You must talk to the Seducer about that. You digress.' He was off again, a proud father showing off junior to the neighbours. 'Once the experiment is complete the crew return through the Sext heat shield, batten down the hatches, and climb up to the cockpit. They then remove the two ladders which fold into the outer casing of the capsule's neck. The capsule performs a normal automatic turn round and drops out of orbit with the capsule heat shield first. Immediately the re-entry is completed the Sext rocket fires and the first astronaut takes control of the machine.'

'And it handles like an ordinary aircraft?'

'It's initially a little fast, but once control is fully regained Sext is very easy to handle.'

'What about handling the capsule itself?'

'Mostly automatic or controlled from the ground. They must have no distractions for the Seducer's experiment.'

'Quite a doddle.'

The Sorcerer looked puzzled. 'Excuse? What is doddle?'

'Like when you're free-wheeling.' Boysie intent on getting the Sorcerer as bemused as the foreigner who, after struggling with the English pronunciation of words like 'cough' and 'bough', committed suicide on seeing a movie poster which proclaimed, THE LIQUIDATOR – PRONOUNCED SUCCESS.

'Free-wheeling. I see.' The Sorcerer obviously did not see.

'What about the engines?' asked Boysie rapidly turning the conversation back to the matter at hand.

'Engines? On Sext you mean?'

'Yes. How do you provide thrust for Sext?'

'Initial thrust is given by a centrally placed YLR99-RM-1 Turborocket. Very interesting because it is throttleable which means you can bring it back to idling before putting in the two CF700 Turbofans.'

'So it gets blown free from the nodule by a turborocket, then uses a pair of turbofans for normal flight.'

'Correct. But come over here to the mock-up and see for yourself.' As they reached the mock-up a voice hailed them from the entrance.

'This is where I find you, hu?' said the Seducer, looking more rodent-like than ever in a thick woollen turtleneck. He came across to them.

'You like the Sorcerer's Sext then, Apprentice?' He looked hard at Boysie.

'Fascinated,' said Boysie returning the hard look while internally his guts seemed to have been set upon by a troop of Boy Scouts learning to tie sheepshanks.

'What can we do for you then?' the Sorcerer chimed in.

'Just lend me your Apprentice for the rest of the morning. I must have him medically examined.'

'Is Yetsofar . . . ?'

'Sonya and Yetsofar are both fine. I pray that Sonya

125

remains that way, but I must at least take the precaution of having a back-up ready for Yetsofar. I get very nervous now.'

'I know. There is a lot at stake. I, too, am concerned. Better safe than sorry.'

'You come with me then.' The Seducer turned to Boysie. 'We should finish by lunchtime. After lunch the Sorcerer will explain the intricacies of flying Sext.'

'Flying what?' Boysie momentarily mis-heard. 'Oh yes, how to fly Sext. I thought you said something really devastating.'

Another G/S Landrover waited outside. A triangular pennant was attached to the bonnet. This carried one word in white against a blue backing. *Seducer*, said the pennant.

'You have your own personal transport, then,' said Boysie trying to sound impressed.

'Naturally. I am the genius behind this operation.'

'Can you tell me . . . ?' Boysie began questioningly. 'What my part of the operation is to be?' The Seducer turned his head towards Boysie. Not a hint of humour showing on his nasty little face. The Landrover was now heading for the cinder track over which Boysie had been driven on the way out.

'Yes, your part of the experiment,' Boysie nodded in affirmation.

The Seducer seemed to be thinking. Finally he said, 'No. I do not think you yet need to know. But I will fill in certain details. The count-down will take roughly twenty-four hours. We should be ready for count-down by tomorrow afternoon.'

'As soon as that?'

'Maybe sooner. Anyway, this means that the two astronauts will go on board at lift-off minus one-twenty minutes.'

'Astronauts?' Boysie stressed the plural.

'Yes, there are two. One American and one Russian. For them the critical stage will be between lift-off minus twenty-four hours until lift-off minus one-twenty minutes. Ideally I should have back-ups, what do you call them? Reserves?'

'Yes.' The word came out slowly, vomity, as Boysie began to see his role in the plan. 'You mean I'm to be a reserve?'

'The ideal would be to have two reserves. You see we must use people who are expendable in case of accidents.'

'So I'm expendable?'

'Certainly. Can you give me one reason why you should be preserved? Have you any unique talent to give to the world?'

'I'm unique for Chrissake.'

'You are a puny middle-aged scientist. A junior at that, by your own admission. To be a junior at your age is a signature on your death sentence. Anyway, whoever carries out this experiment *will* come back. They have to. If I had to use you, you might be very pleased with the result. You would certainly have fame and possibly fortune.'

Fame and fortune were two words always calculated to calm Boysie. On this occasion they only offered mild sedation.

'As I said,' continued the Seducer, 'it would be ideal to have reserve astronauts for both. It is one thing about the planning that I do not like. It should have been taken into consideration, especially as we are not using trained astronauts for the experiment.'

'You're going to shoot people up in space, up above clouds, without training them?'

'As long as their health is moderately good there is little danger. The whole technical operation is controlled from the ground. The pair will have plenty on their minds. My experiment will occupy them almost totally.

The only real training required will be for handling the lifting body, Sext, after re-entry.'

'Well what is the experiment? And who've you conned into taking part?'

The Seducer allowed his pointed face to screw up in a manner which suggested he was smiling. 'We have one Russian and one American. You will back-up the American. If you have to go, the balance will still be good. One Russian and one Englander.'

'What about the Russian then?'

'I do not know what we will do if the Russian gets ill. But at least I will have covered myself if the American goes down. It could happen. They are both a little nervous.'

'I'm not bloody surprised.'

The headquarters came in sight again.

'You will now undergo a pretty exhaustive medical,' said the Seducer as the Landrover came to a standstill. 'That should take you until lunchtime. After lunch you must be briefed on handling Sext. If anything goes wrong with the American I think we can train you fairly quickly for my experiment.' He contorted his face again. To Boysie it had the effect normally only observed in crazy mirrors at the fairground. Sighing deeply, and with desperate nervous tremors, Boysie followed the Seducer into the building. It seemed as though the only possible chance for him to find out about the project was some plague visiting the American astronaut. And what might follow was really unthinkable.

There were two doctors. The first, a sallow sliver of a man, dealt solely with Boysie's body. Eyes, ears, nose, throat, chest, blood pressure, reflexes, clinical history and . . .

'Urinate in that would you,' said the doctor pointing to a tall measuring jar sitting lone and happy on a shelf across the room.

'From here?' Boysie asked frivolously.

The doctor gave him a 'Me-make-heap-bad medicine' look. Boysie wilted and obeyed to the best of his ability.

There followed an X-ray and the dreaded electro-cardiograph which proved to be difficult, Boysie's chest being abnormally hairy, thus making it almost impossible to keep the suckers in place.

If the general medical gave Boysie a certain amount of trouble, he certainly was not prepared for the next doctor. Here he was placed face to face with a smooth-faced, chubby man sporting such a heavy Germanic accent that he sounded like a standard Nazi commandant from any British B movie.

'Just sit down here. That is good. We talk now, *ja*?'

'*Ja* . . . er . . . yes.' Boysie squirmed in his chair.

'First then let me ask some simple questions about autoeroticism.'

For the next hour Boysie was cross-examined to almost embarrassing degree, about his very private life. Slowly and painstakingly the most incredible information about Boysie's sex life began to emerge. And the doctor did not just confine himself to questions. A complicated electronic apparatus was strapped to Boysie's arm.

'This will test your sexual response to colours, smell, words and many other things,' said the doctor.

'I wouldn't have thought it was my arm you needed to fix it to.' Boysie now totally surrendering himself to the charade.

It was one o'clock before the medics let him go. Both the Sorcerer and Seducer were waiting for him. The Seducer left to confer with the doctors while Boysie was piloted to a comfortable and pleasantly situated canteen. The food was not bad by institutional standards and Boysie, together with the Sorcerer, sat at a table marked *Reserved for Senior Personnel and their Assistants*. They were joined by Solomon who did not seem inclined to talk. Boysie glowered in Solomon's direction, hatred welling up as he again heard Constanza's final scream. Solomon's presence at least fortified Boysie's determination to sabotage progress on Wizard.

The Seducer arrived next.

'All right?' asked the Sorcerer with raised eyebrows.

'Very good indeed.' The Seducer again went into his facial contortions. 'In some ways he is better suited than Yetsofar.'

'Indeed,' commented the Sorcerer archly.

At that moment there was a slight stir at the far end of the canteen. The dozen or so guards and technical staff stopped eating to look at the door. A small group of people had entered, the most striking being a young woman. Even with her body part hidden by the blue coveralls which she wore, Boysie recognized a really splendid lady. She was tall, leggy one would suppose, an oval face framed with long blonde hair hanging untidily round her shoulders. She walked with the confidence of a model combined with a natural sensuality. It was as though *Vogue* and *Playboy* had got together and, between them, produced the amalgamated woman. Boysie found he was holding his breath.

The girl was escorted by a wardress-type female, almost a carbon copy of the one who had led Constanza away to death.

Behind the pair walked a guard accompanying a tall and equally beautiful young man, a rare piece of beefcake with cropped blond hair and a body which did not shout at you with aggressive muscles. He looked clear eyed, tanned and wholesome as rye bread and corned beef hash.

The man and the woman were escorted to the table. Once they were seated opposite each other, the wardress and the guard stood back.

'Good morning. Are you well?' The Seducer addressed them in English.

The couple nodded politely but did not speak.

'I must introduce you to my apprentice. Apprentice, meet Sonya and Yetsofar, this is the Sorcerer's Apprentice.'

The girl inclined her head with a grave little smile.

'Hi-ya buddy,' said Yetsofar.

'They are . . . ?' Boysie began.

'Our astronauts,' said the Seducer. 'Sonya is from Tiflis, Georgia, USSR. And Yetsofar comes from Atlanta, Georgia, USA.' Then turning to Sonya and Yetsofar. 'The Sorcerer's Apprentice has been briefed concerning the Sorcerer's part in the operation. No more. You will be circumspect when conversing with him.'

They nodded and immediately put their circumspection to the test by not speaking to Boysie. Boysie tried, vainly, to strike up some kind of a friendship with Yetsofar, who was seated next to him, without success.

After the meal, the astronauts were led away by their respective guards.

'You keep a tight rein on them,' said Boysie to the Sorcerer as they walked towards the main entrance of the complex where the inevitable Landrover was waiting to take them out to the launch site. 'One has to be careful,' agreed von Humperdinck.

Twenty minutes later they were in the Sorcerer's hangar.

'I must now give you the handling instructions for Sext,' smiled the Sorcerer, pleased once more at this opportunity to display his triumph. 'All we really need to do is run over the instruments and controls.' Then, as though a terrible problem had struck him. 'You do fly don't you? Of course, you would not be in the Simulator business if you couldn't fly.'

'Fly?' said Boysie, gritting his teeth. 'Me? Like a bird, Sorcerer, like a bloody bird.'

'Of course.'

'Like a damn great shithawk,' muttered Boysie below his breath. For a second he remembered the one terrifying time when he had, alone and unaided except for orders from a ground control, piloted an aircraft to safety. Now, near to the possibility of doing it again, his stomach began a hesitation roll. True he knew the simple things, like if you pushed the stick forward you went down, backwards you went up, unless you did not have enough power, from side to side you dipped the wings in a bank, while pushing on the foot pedals took you in the direction you wished to go. But that was about all.

'Come, then let's get you into the cockpit.'

'Cockpit,' mused Boysie. 'More like a cock-up.'

Humperdinck helped him into the pilot's seat. The whole cockpit was surprisingly wide, controls on the left, and a battery of instruments. Plenty of room in the right hand seat for a passenger. Climbing in beside Boysie, Humperdinck first showed him how to lock the canopy.

'The flying controls are normal,' he continued. 'As are the flight instruments. The panel directly in front of you, as you can see, is standard, except that the instruments are from different countries of origin. We try to get the best. To the left you have the Machmeter; she will exceed speeds of Mach 3, of course. Engine instruments to the right. Throttle control for the turborocket marked in red, on the centre pedestal, below that the twin throttles for the turbofans marked yellow. Flaps and trim on the left of the pedestal.'

Boysie sat back, at least he could identify the throttles and flaps. That would be a help.

'Gear selector, up or down, under the dash towards the centre. Three warning lights just above it.' Humperdinck went on oblivious of Boysie's incomprehension. 'Now, as well as the standard altimeter, you will notice there are two vertical altimeters, graded in feet and miles. Also, on either side of the panel you have a radio altimeter, these are the dual altimeters which work in connection with a highly developed automatic landing devise based on the Bendix Precision Approach and Landing System.'

'Really?' Boysie still keeping his end up.

'Yes, very interesting. You have an autopilot coupler, which locks on to the ILS beacon amplifier coupler, the dual radio altimeters, two flare computers, a standby gyro-horizon, yaw damper and monitors to check the operation of the auto-pilot and instruments. And, of course, there is the automatic throttle control.'

'Of course.' Boysie grinned.

'See,' said Humperdinck leaning over the controls and pointing out the instruments. 'There you have the approach control panel, approach and progress display, first and second low range radio altimeters; autopilot and throttle warning lights. Simple.'

'You mean I just flick this switch and it all happens?'

'First catch your airfield, Apprentice, eh?'

'Yes.' Boysie prayed he would never be called to operate the infernal machine.

He spent the remainder of the afternoon going through the various drills, concerning Sext. It was interesting enough, thought Boysie, but it certainly did not put him in a stronger position concerning sabotage. He worried at the situation all through dinner. Sonya and Yetsofar joined them again, and again they remained stolidly silent.

At nine-thirty the Sorcerer escorted him back to his room. There followed the same routine as on the previous night. His door was locked from the outside and there followed the snuffling and scratching of a dog.

It was a long time before Boysie got to sleep. And even then his slumber was far from sound. The terror nightmares began to trick his mind. He was in the pilot's seat of Sext going at an enormous speed. Next to him sat Constanza, her head turned away from him. The ground was coming up fast, then, from nowhere, the killer Alsatians were scratching on the canopy trying to get in. Constanza turned towards him, but her face was only a skull, empty sockets where her eyes should be. Behind her the dog was changing form. A man. Solomon was knocking on the canopy. Softly knocking . . . knocking . . . knocking. Boysie woke in a sweat, shaking. A dream? No, the knocking went on. Coming from the window, a soft steady knocking. Boysie swallowed, got out of bed and slowly crossed to the window. The knocking still continued. Another swallow and he clutched at the curtains, pulling them back.

CHAPTER EIGHT

SILVERSMITH

The Silversmith has tarnished hands,
A tarnished mind and tarnished heart.
GOLD AND THE LIKE: Granger Carroll

THE duty sergeant had a hard job waking Mostyn. James George Mostyn, unlike Brian Ian (Boysie) Oakes did not dream in technicolor. His dreams, like his waking hours, were clean-cut in black and white. At six in the morning he had just entered the bedroom of a young female cinematograph performer, truth forbade one to describe her as an actress. But she was well known, particularly in Mostyn's dreams. A large part of his sleeping hours were spent in her company. But the present six o'clock dream would not finish true to form. Mostyn held out his arms to the female, woke and found himself reaching for a sergeant.

'The General and some other officers will meet you in the gymnasium at six-thirty, sir.'

'Whasamatter. General. What . . .' Then, as consciousness flooded back, 'what the hell? What's the bloody time?'

'Five after six, sir.'

'In the morning?' blinked Mostyn in disbelief.

'In the morning, sir. You are operational tonight. Remember, sir?'

Mostyn remembered gloomily. 'Yes. Where's the gym?'

'Not far, sir. I'm to take you over. Nice cup of hot tea here, sir.'

Mostyn looked at the dark brown brew as though it was an unpleasant happening on the table. He ran his fingers through his tight wiry hair and shook his head as if to sweep sleep away.

'All right, sar'nt. Wait outside.'

The duty sergeant left, and, with ill grace, Mostyn showered and shaved, throwing out regular mental curses concerning the day when he had first met Boysie.

Walking from the comparative warmth of the officers' quarters into the open air was like plunging into a pool of iced water. The air nearly froze Mostyn's lungs, and he was decidedly out of breath by the time they reached the gymnasium.

The General was waiting with four other officers.

'Ah. Colonel Mostyn.' He was a man of sardonic wit and terrifying vocal ferocity. When the General spoke it was like being hit in the face with a wet kipper. Mostyn took a step back as the force of the greeting reached him.

'Nice to have you here,' the General continued. 'Gentlemen, this is Colonel Mostyn. Fine operational record with Intelligence. Second-in-Command of Special Security until he retired last year. Volunteered to sign on again and help us out of the present bit of trouble.'

Mostyn inclined his head in mock modesty. Lifting his eyes he found himself locked in the General's gaze. He could read the satire in the senior officer's eyes. He knew damn well that Mostyn had been press-ganged into the job. And he knew that Mostyn knew he knew. A wicked conspiracy of silence passed between the two men while the other officers stood suitably overawed by the whole business.

'Now,' shrieked the General. 'If we're going to get Colonel Mostyn off tonight there's a lot to be done. Leave you in the tender hands of these officers and we'll talk later.' He gave a curt nod and strode out of the gymnasium, purposefully, towards bacon, eggs, coffee and toast.

For a second, Mostyn had a mental picture of the remaining officers advancing on him, while he backed away muttering, 'No . . . no . . . no . . .' It did not quite happen like that, but Mostyn was soon swept into a whirlpool of military techniques which he thought he had left behind many years before.

A parachute training instructor went over all the elementary lessons, Mostyn digging back into his memory, recalling things like critical speeds, oscillation and squidding.

By mid-morning Mostyn was really struggling. This time with a brutish PTI, brushing up on unarmed combat and its allied sciences. 'And don't forget, sir,' barked the PTI, 'never hit a man when he's down. Just kick him.' It was a nostalgic phrase which Mostyn himself had used many times when lecturing to recruits at the Special Security training centre.

Before lunch, they helped him into parachute harness, bundled him into one of the Albatross amphibians and then made him leap from the skies in the first parachute jump he had made since the forties.

After lunch, Mostyn was faced with kitting out. Stores provided him with the bare essentials; K rations, compass and a small personal medical kit. The General had insisted that Mostyn should choose the more warlike kit himself. He already carried the small transistorized direction finder pack which would lead him to Boysie's electronic shoes. He also carried his own personal survival kit, consisting of a half-litre flask of brandy, the omnipotent jalap, toilet paper, a bottle of travel sickness pills and a leather-bound copy of *War and Peace* which he intended to read one day.

He chose a French TR-PP-11 subminiature radio rigged for fixed frequency transmission. Later, at the briefing, he was given times when there would be a listening aircraft within range.

For protection Mostyn signed for a short bladed fighting knife and chose a Smith and Wesson 399 mm automatic and ten magazines. He eschewed the Weather PPK on grounds of snobbery, but, as though to make up for it, he added one torch and one Polaroid 104 Land Camera to his possessions.

The General and his officers had gone to town for the briefing, providing a three dimensional model of the island which had been hastily prepared, following a careful high altitude photoreconnaissance that morning.

The photographs had picked up an area which could possibly be a launch pad, four tracks large enough to be roughly made up roads, and an E-shaped building which definitely showed signs of habitation.

The pilot who was to drop Mostyn that night gave a brief summary of the problems involved. If they were going to get away undetected it meant flying in very low, to avoid radar, cutting the engines during the run over the island, dispatching Mostyn at around 600 feet, and not opening up again until they were almost down to fifty feet. The pilot and his crew had been trying it out over the sea that morning and were reasonably confident. Mostyn showed his usual indifference, yet, to his chagrin, found his hands trembling noticeably when he lit a cigarette.

There followed two hours' conversation which covered radio procedure, what strength Mostyn could call down on the island if he felt it was safe enough not to incur the wrath of Russia, code signs, call signs and all the usual mumbo-jumbo of a military operation.

The briefing over, Mostyn retired to his quarters. At eleven, they wakened him. He dressed in battledress over arctic underwear, and a camouflage jacket. In the mess a hot meal awaited him. Then, an hour later, pockets stuffed with equipment, and hung about like a Christmas tree, Mostyn climbed aboard the waiting Albatross. Within ten minutes they were off into the wide black yonder, heading, Mostyn hoped, for an appointment with Boysie. At least, he thought as they thundered through the sky, he could play the hero with Griffin and Chicory when he got back. If he got back. Mostyn began to worry, for the first time, about the outcome of his mission.

The air was bitterly cold and Mostyn was surrounded by unaccustomed silence. The aircraft roar had dropped to a wild and frightening whisper as the pilot cut his engines and put the nose down towards the island. Mostyn had crouched in the doorway waiting for the dispatcher to bang him on the shoulder, the signal for him to leap out into the unknown. It came sooner than he expected, and Mostyn now found himself drifting towards an earth which he could not see. A mile or so away to his left there were lights, then the earth rushed up, unexpectedly, and he was rolling over and over.

Now, Mostyn stood in the silence, gathering in the shroud lines of his parachute, and allowing his eyes to become accustomed to the dark. He had landed on hard, slightly rocky, tundra, far too hard for him to dig a hole in which he could bury the parachute, so he had to make do with rolling up the canopy and weighting it down with stones. Cursing the cold, he unbuttoned one of the jacket pockets, drew out the D/F pack and inserted the earphone into his right ear. Switching on, Mostyn turned up the volume and began to move quietly in a circle. There was the crackle of static from the headphone, then, softly and growing louder, the familiar *tweet-twit-twit-twit, tweet-tweet-tweet*. Moving carefully in a sweeping arc, Mostyn aligned himself with the point from which the loudest signal seemed to be coming, then, hand on the Smith and Wesson, he moved forward. The signal got louder and louder. Two or three times Mostyn stumbled on the uneven ground. Then, he saw the lights ahead. The signal seemed to be coming from the heart of the lights. Slowly he crept nearer. The signal was more distinct now. Ahead the outlines of a building showed harshly symmetrical against the sky. Drawing the automatic, Mostyn made a quick run towards the building, flattening himself against its wall. The tweet and twitting of the D/F grew louder and began to merge together. Stealthily Mostyn moved along the wall. The signal merged completely into an earsplitting whine. Mostyn dragged the earphone from his head. He was standing by a window. Either Boysie or his shoes were behind the heavy double-glazing. Gently, Mostyn began to tap the glass.

Boysie dragged back the curtains, his heart thumping like a bass drum. Outside, a face leered up at him. Boysie felt his hair streak upwards and his heart trip a beat. He peered closer. The figure outside seemed to be signalling. It was trying to tell him something. The figure was searching for something. Suddenly it found what it was after. A torch. The small beam of light lit up the intruder's face. Mostyn stood outside Boysie's window. It took a good half-minute for the truth to sink in. Then Boysie was fumbling with the heavy window-catches. A blast of icy air swept into the room as the window pivoted on its central retaining pins.

'Taken your time, haven't you?' whispered Mostyn. 'You're absolutely certain I can come in?'

'Feel free,' said Boysie, still thinking this was a dream.

Mostyn clambered in and, together, they swung the window back in place.

'For chrissake keep quiet,' muttered Boysie. 'How the hell did you get here anyway? And how the hell did you find me?'

'Time for that later.' Mostyn looked round. 'How safe are we?'

'You must have had your Joan the Wad or St Christopher medal working overtime,' said Boysie. 'They've got the building protected by dog patrols. Mad dog patrols. Bloody killer Alsatians.'

'How safe are we here?'

'There's a bloody great mad killer Alsatian outside the door, that's all. I suppose they thought it unlikely that I'd try and make a run for it. Especially after the dog got Constanza. I say?' He looked up quite perky. 'Don't suppose you brought Chicory along?'

'I did not bring Chicory along.'

'Griffin?'

'They are both on their way back to London with any luck. Anywhere here I can hide?'

'There's the closet.' Boysie pointed to the big built-in cupboard. 'No one goes near that as far as I know.'

'All right, I'll use it when the time comes.' Mostyn had the cupboard doors open and was trying it for size. 'Now what the hell's been going on here?'

Boysie took a deep breath and launched into the story of his life from the seasick morning aboard the *Warbash Admiral* right up to the strange project on Wizard.

'So you don't really know what is happening?' queried Mostyn.

'Not really. Only what I've told you. They're going to test this lifting body, but that looks like its only an aside. Two astronauts male and female, and . . .'

'And you, Boysie,' said Mostyn with a gluttonous smile, 'are the reserve male.'

'Oh no. I've done a lot of things for you in my time but I'm not going to put my arse under a bloody great rocket for you or anybody.'

'Worry not, little Oaksie, worry not.' It was the old sly Mostyn again. 'Just think about it. We don't know the full strength of what's going on here. You've already told me that you don't think there are any Russian troops on the island. I can call in a strike only when I'm certain of the facts. So, all you have to do is get yourself picked to play the juvenile lead in this drama.'

'And let them light the blue paper under me?'

'Yes.'

'Not bloody likely.'

'List, list, oh, list, laddie. There is no need to let them even light the blue paper. Once you know what is going on, you will also be appraised of the launch time.'

'So?'

'So I can call in a strike before they get anywhere near the old five-four-three-two-one bit.'

Boysie creased his brow, making his thinking face.

'How?' he said finally with a smug grin, 'how am I going to get old Yetsofar out of the race?'

Mostyn chuckled. 'Uncle thinks of everything, old son. Everything.' His hand came up. In it was clutched the bottle of jalap.

'And how am I going to feed it to him?'

'Your problem, Boysie. Your problem. You eat with them don't you? Make your opportunity, lad. That's real strategy for you.'

Boysie nodded sadly. He should have known better. One just did not win when Mostyn was playing.

'Another thing,' continued Mostyn. 'You say you do not recognize the fellow who calls himself the Seducer?'

'Not a clue. And they're bringing in this bloke today. The Silversmith. Mr bloody Midas.'

'I wonder,' said Mostyn who, for all his sliminess, had an incredible memory for faces. When he worked for the Department they used to say that Mostyn rarely had to refer to the ID book. He carried it all in his head. 'Wonder if it would work?'

'You know it rotten works,' said Boysie looking at the little jalap bottle.

'Not that. Look, lad, do you think you could use this.' Mostyn brought out the Polaroid camera like a magician revealing the chosen card.

'I suppose so. Could hide it under me parka and . . .'

'And await the right moment. You do that, son, you do that. You know how the thing works?'

'Got one of my own back home,' said Boysie airily. 'Hope you've got a cold clip for that one. Won't get any decent pictures in this climate if you haven't.'

'Everything's here. Black and white film pack, the lot. Just try and get me some pictures of the lecherous Seducer and his pal the Silversmith and we'll see if my brain can do the rest.'

'And you want Yetsofar spiked. Nothing else I can do for you while I'm at it?'

'Yes. You might find out why they need such a bloody great rocket. The *Saturn V* is the launch vehicle for the moon you know.'

It was nearly dawn. Boysie helped Mostyn to make himself comfortable in the closet. Once he had Mostyn stowed away with his K rations and bits and pieces, Boysie shaved and prepared himself. The Sorcerer had said he would be round to pick up Boysie at eight. He dressed as far as the coverall, then slipped the carrying strap of the camera around his neck before donning the parka.

The Sorcerer arrived promptly at eight, delighted to see Boysie up. They breakfasted together and, like the previous day, took a Landrover ride down to the launch site.

'We should be able to start the count down around two o'clock this afternoon,' said the Seducer, looking pleased with himself.

'Oh yes. And what time do Sonya and Yetsofar go aboard?'

'Oh, two hours from lift off. About noon tomorrow providing all goes well. But come, we must go through the lessons you learned yesterday.'

Humperdinck prattled on with Boysie making yes noises. Then, at eleven, the loudspeaker system clamoured into action. 'The countdown will begin at noon. Will the Sorcerer go to the main entrance, please. Silversmith's aircraft landed.' The detached voice repeated the message twice.

'Ah. I am in demand.' The Sorcerer leaped up and down with glee. 'The Silversmith is here.'

'Do I come too?' asked Boysie.

'They haven't asked for you. But I take you with me. As far as the entrance anyway.'

The main hangar was deserted. The technicians had spirited the space capsule away. At the main entrance, the Sorcerer motioned to Boysie with his hand. 'You stay here. The Seducer is playing god today and I expect the Silversmith will be in the same vein. Better for you to stay where you are.'

Boysie nodded and allowed the Sorcerer to pass up the passage towards the main personnel doors. Counting to ten Boysie unzipped his parka and brought out the Polaroid camera. Flicking down the outer case he extended the bellows and lifted the viewfinder into position. Strangely he felt little fear as he crept up the passage towards the light.

Boysie halted just short of the glass doors through which he could see the Sorcerer and Seducer with Solomon and three of the goons with the white roundels on their backs.

Creeping forward, Boysie pushed the doors half open and began to get the group in focus. He sensed movement somewhere to the left. Seconds later a Landrover pulled into his view. A man descended from the Landrover and shook hands briefly with the Seducer and Sorcerer. Then, the Silversmith, short and immaculate even in a parka, turned towards the door. For a second, Boysie had the three men fully in focus. He squeezed the trigger, turned, and ran back down the passage. He was in the Sorcerer's workshop, with the camera out of sight under his parka, long before the trio entered the hangar.

Boysie heard their footsteps echoing as they came across the cold concrete of the hangar. Strangely he felt slight trepidation at the prospect of meeting the Silversmith. Possibly because, Solomon apart, the Silversmith was the one man who might not accept him on face value.

They came into the Sorcerer's workshop as though in a kind of formation. The Silversmith ahead, Seducer and Sorcerer on either side slightly to the rear. Solomon behind, like a tail end Charlie.

'This him?' The Silversmith had a voice which might have cut through steel, it was edged with authority, the kind of voice used to quell storms, or create them. He was much shorter than Boysie, yet his physical presence instantly commanded attention. The Silversmith stood directly in front of Boysie and threw back the hood of his parka displaying a fine head of silver hair, so silver that it looked almost phoney. Perhaps it was a clue to the man's character.

'Yes, this is him,' said the Seducer.

'You know who I am?' The man addresssed Boysie.

'You're the . . . the Silversmith.'

'Ten out of bloody ten. And what does the Silversmith do?'

'You provide the money for this operation.'

'I do, do I?'

'That's what they told me.'

'And they're right.' He turned to Solomon. 'If he's harmless all well and good. Slightest trouble or hint of trouble.' The Silversmith drew his hand across his neck. Solomon nodded, a grizzly affirmative.

145

'Money I provide, eh?' The Silversmith was addressing Boysie again. 'Yes, I provide money, but only a fool would put money into a venture like this without insuring himself. I put money in so that the project will make money. I don't know who you are, or why. The Sorcerer seems to trust you. Solomon does not. But you will have noticed that. Remember it because Solomon is my man.' He paused to let it sink in. 'Then,' he continued. 'The Seducer is not quite certain about you. I have an open mind. Time will tell.' He spoke the last words as if they formed some great and witty epigram. All they did was to serve as a full stop to the conversation. With a quick motion to Solomon, the Silversmith turned on his heel and began to march purposefully towards the exit leading to the main hangar.

As the footsteps died away the Seducer said. 'I had better join him in launch control. You and your Apprentice go to lunch.'

The Sorcerer nodded and wagged his head at Boysie. 'We go,' was all he said.

'How do you think I made out with the Silversmith?' asked Boysie as the Landrover sped them back to the Headquarters Building.

'He is a very astute man. He judges people by the work they do. We, as scientists, recognize you immediately as one of us. But with the Silversmith it is more difficult.'

Boysie overawed by being told he looked like a scientist, nodded sagely. 'Think I'll freshen up a little before lunch,' he said when they reached the building.

'Good. I wait for you in the dining hall.' The Sorcerer smiled.

Back in his room, Boysie unlocked the closet to find Mostyn sitting inside, cross legged and dozing.

'Having a spot of the old transcendentals then?' he said cheerfully.

'Merely meditating on the follies of this planet and its

inhabitants,' said Mostyn pompously. 'You get the photo?'

'Yes, but I haven't much time.' Boysie had unzipped his parka and taken the camera from round his neck. Mostyn grabbed the instrument tore off the first label and wrenched the photograph out. 'Quick. I've got the clip,' muttered Boysie. Mostyn handed the photograph to him, backing still intact. Boysie swiftly slipped it into the cold clip which had been nestling in an inside pocket of his coveralls all morning.

Ten seconds later, they removed the photograph and tore off the backing. It was a tolerably good print. 'How about that then? How about that?' Boysie preened.

'All right, proper little Lord Snowdon. Let's see.'

Boysie pointed out the figures. 'That's Humperdinck, the Sorcerer, this fellow's the Seducer. One in the middle is the Silversmith, Solomon's bringing up the rear.'

'Solomon!' said Mostyn loudly as though he had been stung. 'You realize what you've done? You've only got the scoop photograph of the year. People have been trying to get friend Solomon's likeness for years. Of course. Solomon. I should have remembered. Who's this one?'

'The Seducer,' said Boisy lamely.

'Funny. His real name's Schneider. Hans Wilhelm Schneider.'

'You sure?'

'Sure I'm sure. I got him for our people. Brought him over the bloody wall that's all. Strange that he should be in on this. He specializes in space biology. Behaviour of plants and animal life in space. Very funny. And I know this joker as well.' Stabbing at the photograph with his forefinger.

'Who? The Silversmith?'

'Quite. The Silversmith. But he has a rather grand name in the City. His name's Sir Bruce Gravestone. I only know because his picture was all over the front pages last week. Just sold out a vast shareholding. Said he was leaving to live in the Bahamas or somewhere.'

'He may be doing just that, once they've made some loot out of this.'

'Pop me back in the cupboard, Boysie, and set about your mate Yetsofar with the jalap.' Mostyn was already settling himself on the floor. Boysie closed the door, turned on the key and put his hand into his inside pocket to clutch the tiny bottle of laxative.

Feeding the lethal mixture to Yetsofar was easier than he expected. The Sorcerer had already taken his seat at the reserved table in the dining hall when Boysie arrived. So were the intrepid space hero and heroine, Sonya and Yetsofar. The place next to Yetsofar was vacant. Better still it was on the outside, the side from which food was passed up the table. Boysie, watched and waited. The moment came when the fruit salad came. With a magnificent piece of palming Boysie grasped a dish containing one portion of fruit salad and, at the same time held the phial of jalap, uncorked in the palm of his hand. He used the oldest dodge in the business as misdirection. Bringing the dish of salad in line with his chest, he put on a puzzled expression, staring towards the door on the far side of the room. As he started to pass the dish on, Boysie still staring, let out a low 'Who is that?'

Yetsofar, Sonya and the Sorcerer all turned and looked in the direction of Boysie's gaze. In a flash, Boysie dropped the dish on to the table and slipped his hand over it to allow the contents of the phial to drop into the salad. By the time Yetsofar turned back to the table, the dish of fruit salad was there in front of him. He ate the lot.

Just before two in the afternoon the Sorcerer was leading Boysie to the main entrance yet again, prattling on about the count down and using incredible technicalities. The monologue passed over Boysie's head. He merely nodded and said 'yes' and 'naturally' when it seemed best. As they reached the foyer, in sight of the Landrover waiting outside, the loudspeaker system let out its shriek. The shrill whine died. The Sorcerer stood still.

'Sorcerer and Apprentice to Launch Lecture Room One.' The Loudspeaker gave the order twice before the Sorcerer broke into a double.

'Something drastic has happened,' said the Sorcerer as he reached the Landrover.

'For instance?' yelled Boysie, climbing in beside him.

'For instance with the count down or something.'

The Landrover set off at a speed which made the vehicle bounce and roll so that, to the passengers, it gave a passable simulation of what life was like bronco busting.

The Seducer and Silversmith stood outside the low building a couple of hundred yards from the launch pad. They turned and walked slowly down the steps and into the building as the Landrover drew up. Boysie followed the Sorcerer from the vehicle into the building.

It was a simple bare room with wooden folding chairs marshalled in neat rows facing a raised dais and a blackboard wall.

At the blackboard end stood the Silversmith, Seducer and Solomon. In the front row, her back to the door, sat Sonya.

'Good,' the Seducer called out. 'The Sorcerer's Apprentice is being elevated to a more lofty station.'

'So what's wrong?' The Sorcerer looked puzzled.

'Yetsofar,' said the Seducer crisply. 'Yetsofar has been taken ill. The doctor has diagnosed food poisoning of a particularly virile nature. You are all right?' He looked at Boysie.

'Fine. Never better,' said Boysie with a sheepish grin.

'You will have to be fit. You will now take Yetsofar's

place. Come. Come and sit next to Sonya, your partner on this venture. A partner in more ways than one.'

Sonya turned and looked at Boysie as though he was the only man in the room.

It had worked, but now Boysie began to feel misgivings. The old lusts of escape stirred inside him and he returned Sonya's look with a dividend of lechery.

CHAPTER NINE

SONYA

So Sonya, like a leaf
Was borne into the heady air,
And thus did come and keep her tryst
With Olaf brave and fair.
THE MATING OF OLAF: Trans. by Sigmund Dross

'COME and sit next to me.' Sonya's voice had a smouldering texture.

'Sure,' said Boysie, swallowing and edging in.

'Good, it is necessary that you should get acquainted.' The Seducer was smiling. A lascivious smile. Almost a full-blooded drool.

It was not usual for Boysie to blush, but somehow the atmosphere and Sonya's unspoken words made him colour up.

'You approve, Sonya?' asked the Sorcerer.

Sonya lifted a hand and brushed back an exquisite fall of hair. 'Of course I approve. Naturally I am sad about Yetsofar. He was a truly magnificent creature.' She turned her head and looked at Boysie, scrutinizing him as a farmer will examine a horse. The blush on Boysie's cheeks became more pronounced. 'Yet, looking at this one,' she continued, 'it might turn out even better than we hoped.'

'You realize,' the Seducer was facing Sonya, 'that a great deal will depend on you now.'

'My apprentice will handle Sext,' the Sorcerer interposed.

'I'm sure he can.' The Seducer said. 'I am worrying a little about the mechanics of the capsule.'

'There is no need for worry. I have had your training. It is all that is necessary.' Sonya gave a pout in Boysie's direction.

'God help you, young woman, if anything goes wrong, then.' The Silversmith took a pace forward into the group. 'That goes for all of you. I haven't poured money into this concern for nothing and it strikes me you've already ridden near to disaster, courted it even. So, if anything happens to upset the plans, like old Shylock I'll have my pound of flesh. From each one of you.' He gave a brusque motion with his hand in Solomon's direction, indicating that he wanted the man to come with him. 'You'd better get your new boy briefed. While we run over the method of extracting the largest amount from the highest bidder.' Hands behind his back, the Silversmith stalked from the room. Solomon in his wake.

There was an embarrassed silence, eventually broken by the Seducer.

'To work, then, to work.' Even the Seducer sounded less confident after locking metaphorical horns with the Silversmith. 'Sonya, this gentleman knows only half of the experiment. The half with the lifting body.'

'He has a pleasant surprise in store then.' She turned to Boysie. 'That is if you don't find me repellent.'

'Repellent?' said Boysie, speaking in the upper register. 'You, repellent? I'd say just the opposite.'

'It will make things easier.' She smiled a full-blown summer smile, the kind of smile that Boysie remembered from his youth, when there was sport among the village girls, round and round the hayricks and among the Berkshire corn.

'Much easier.' agreed the Seducer turning to Boysie. 'You see the main purpose of the experiment is not simply to check on my friend's lifting body. Your main purpose is to procreate.'

'To do what?' squawked Boysie as though hit by falling masonry.

'Procreate,' said the Sorcerer.

'Procreate,' said the Seducer.

'In your quaint idiomatic English,' said Sonya. 'They mean that you have to get me in the club.'

'In a space capsule?' Boysie spoke weakly.

'That is the whole point,' replied the Seducer. 'You and Sonya must couple while in orbit . . .'

'I've heard of flying high but this is ridiculous,' said Boysie, still blushing crimson.

The Seducer shook his head in a distinct negative. 'Not ridiculous. You and Sonya will be founder members of the new race. The space babies. The sky children. It is an exciting project, yes?'

Boysie gabbled unintelligibly. At last he got out, 'If you bloody well think I'm going to be tossed round the earth at lord knows how many miles per hour and make love to this lady at the same time you've got another think coming.'

'And so have you, Mr. Oakes.' The Seducer came up close. He smelled of garlic. 'You are being most churlish to the lady. You must not refuse her.'

'I'm not refusing her. I'm just a shade put out.' Boysie decided he had played the coward long enough. Now he would have to cool it slowly. It would be comparatively easy to be a hero. Especially if one knew the rocket would never get off the ground. Old Mostyn would see to that. 'Say I decided to go through with this. What sort of . . . er . . . remuneration would I get?'

'What Yetsofar would have got. Ten per cent of the final price,' said the Sorcerer. 'You see what we are doing? As soon as you are in orbit we put the results up for auction. America, Russia and Great Britain will all bid.

In fact what country wouldn't like to own the first space child and its mother.'

'What about the father?' Boysie indignant.

'You are of little importance once Sonya is impregnated. You can be paid off. Of course if America or Britain win you can be sure of more hard currency from the tabloid newspapers. The story is what I believe they call a natural.'

Boysie chuckled to himself. It would be almost worthwhile going through with it. He could see the headlines. COME OFF IT, MR. OAKES – *Daily Mirror*. MY SECRET ASSIGNATION IN SPACE. AMAZING REVELATIONS – *News of the World*. THIS FILTHY EXPERIMENT IN THE NAME OF SCIENCE – *The People*.

'Okay, start the clock.' Boysie grinned at the Sorcerer and the Seducer, happy in his knowledge that there was no danger.

The two men looked relieved and Sonya stood up to plant a kiss on Boysie's cheek.

'There,' beamed the Sorcerer like a marriage guidance counsellor. 'It is a love match.'

'You are too sentimental.' The Seducer spat. 'This is a scientific experiment. Love matches do not come into it. We must approach this clinically.' He looked at Boysie. 'Now perhaps the medical we gave you on arrival makes sense. We have a very good working knowledge of how you function sexually. We know what smells, words and colours give you stimulus. We also know which are the most sensitive areas of your body. All that information will be passed over to Sonya and a similar dossier, concerning Sonya will be passed to you for perusal.'

Boysie had been looking at Sonya during the last sentences. She returned the look and the physical attraction of male for female and female for male bleeped out between them. Boysie imagined a row of hearts going from head to head like in the comic pictures. He missed the first few words of the Seducer's next sentence.

'. . . the launch and re-entry procedures you already know, what we have to do now is simply give you a more detailed pattern of how the flight will take place and which instruments you need to know within the capsule'.

'Just a minute.' Boysie raised his hand. 'There is one thing I would like to ask. Why, if we are just going into orbit, do you need such a damn great rocket?' He looked at the two German scientists as if to say, caught-you-that-time.

'But I have just been explaining. You obviously don't take this seriously.'

'I do, I do,' chanted Boysie, trying to make good his lapse. 'It's only that I find it difficult. Difficult to adjust to the idea of being shot into space.'

'Well, for your information.' The Seducer sounded every syllable. 'We have to use a very large launch vehicle for two reasons. First, the pay load is considerably heavier than normal. Second, before we can get you into orbit we have to fire you on a low trajectory. This is done by two small computers in the launch vehicle guidance system. The first stage takes you to a point quite near the Tropic of Cancer. Somewhere over India we reckon. Then, as the first stage falls away your direction will be changed . . .'

'To straight up?' said Boysie.

'As you observe, to straight up. The second stage will take you into orbit. The Sorcerer must have already shown you the instruments in Sext which will supply you with information from the capsule during the launch and just prior to re-entry.'

'Yes, he did.' Boysie remembered the panel of lights, and the digital counter, below the flight instruments.

'Good.' The Seducer rubbed his hands. 'Then you must realize there are duplicate instruments in the capsule. So between both sets of instruments you will be told automatically when to go down to the capsule from Sext, and when to make the journey back before re-entry.'

'Don't worry. I show you.' Sonya still smouldered pleasantly. 'As easy as . . .'

'Falling off a log,' Boysie finished.

'Yes,' chorused the brace of scientists.

'Yes,' said Boysie. 'But there are a couple of other things I don't quite understand.'

'Perhaps you will when we go up to the capsule.'

'Maybe. But tell me, and stop me if I'm wrong, I seem to remember that when people go into orbit they have to be dressed up in spacesuits and helmets with damn great visors on them to keep off radiation.'

'So?' The Seducer looked puzzled.

'So, if we're done up in all that gear how the heck are we going to . . . well . . . copulate.'

Gentle chuckles emanated from both the scientists and Sonya.

'It is quite safe,' wheezed the Seducer. 'Once in orbit you can remove all clothing. The warning buzzer for re-entry goes at the start of your final orbit. Probably the fourth orbit. So, as each orbit takes roughly ninety minutes you have that space of time to readjust your clothing.'

'I see,' said Boysie patiently, like a male nurse talking to a ninny. 'Well how about this one. We will, I presume, be in a weightless condition once we're in orbit.'

'Yes.' There was a slight trace of razor's edge in the way the Seducer answered him.

'Well, I should have thought there was an obvious difficulty. I don't see that I need to elaborate on it.' Boysie stopped, looking lamely at the Seducer, waiting for him to say something. The Seducer simply looked straight into Boysie's eyes. 'I mean, how do you . . .' Boysie began. 'How do you . . . er . . . manage it? I mean with being weightless and all that. Everything'll float won't it? Everything?'

'Do you think we are absolute fools.' The Seducer was purple with rage. It was as though someone had disputed his parentage. 'I have spent months, years, preparing for this. You think we didn't take the weightless condition into account? It was the first thing. The very first thing we did was to work out a method by which humans could procreate in a weightless zone. We go up to the capsule now. From there you will be able to see for yourself. And what you do not understand Sonya will teach you.'

Heights were not Boysie's strongpoint. As the lift whipped them up to the capsule towering at twice the height of Nelson's column, Boysie breathed a silent prayer. This was pure madness, even though he knew in his heart of hearts that Mostyn would call down the wrath of NATO upon the island and its strange inhabitants long before the rocket could shift a fraction. It was madness to tempt fate. Fate? Fête? A fête worse than death. Boysie giggled like a schoolgirl as his mind ripped back to the memory of the corny old joke.

The elevator whined to a halt.

'*Unterkleider*,' announced the Sorcerer with a loud guffaw.

'What's he on about?' Boysie whispered to Sonya.

'It's supposed to be a joke. He said we had arrived at the underwear department.' She put out her hand. Their palms met and Boysie felt the delicious tingle up his arm and down the spinal cord.

'What a beautiful way to go,' he said quietly. 'Shot out to infinity with a magnificent female.'

'That is a nice compliment. Yetsofar never paid me compliments. I think I shall like you better.'

'Attagirl. It's just what my old pappy would have wished. After you with the capsule.'

'Take him inside.' The Seducer addressed Sonya. 'I

will listen to what you tell him and correct any errors.'

'There will be no errors, comrade. I do not make mistakes.' Sonya bent low to climb into the capsule. Boysie followed suit and groped his way through the hatch.

To his surprise the interior was roomy. He could almost stand upright while touching one of the two aluminium ladders which reached down from the nose in which Sext was comfortably mated. The bulk of the capsule was taken up with a large, raised and leather-padded couch. Sonya laid herself back on the yielding surface, and motioned to Boysie to lie beside her. On his back, looking straight up, Boysie found himself gazing at a small panel of lights, two digital computers and a small battery of switches.

'You should be able to reach the switches from this position,' said Sonya. 'You see, if all goes well, the two central lights go on and a warning buzzer sounds as we are entering the final orbit. The whole thing is remotely controlled.'

'What if it doesn't operate?'

'If we lose contact, or if anything goes wrong, we can activate the system by manually switching in the guidance computers.' She wagged a hand in the direction of the line of switches. 'The lights will come on, the buzzer will sound and the digital counter goes into operation in exactly the same way as they respond to the remote control. Which ever way it goes we have around ninety minutes to get back into Sext.'

'And what about the experiment in here?' Boysie thought that for a second he detected a slight flush across the Russian girl's face.

'We have to be ingenious,' she said. 'There are the Seducer's aids. Stirrups for my feet and arms.' Sonya indicated the rubber padded half circles at the bottom and top of the couch. 'In this centre piece at the back behind our heads, there are other aids. A weight belt for each of us. Feet weights for you. Lockers in which to stow our clothes and a weighted net to throw over ourselves if necessary. We will manage.'

'Yes,' said Boysie. 'Suppose we will.'

Half an hour and many explanations later, they left the capsule. As the lift dropped them to ground level Boysie asked the Seducer, 'When do we go on board? For real, I mean?'

'If the count down goes on normally you go on board at noon tomorrow. Lift off should be at around fourteen hundred hours.'

'Two o'clock,' Boysie mused, his thoughts trained on Mostyn and his liaison with the NATO people in Spitzbergen. 'One other thing,' he said cheekily. 'How can you be sure that Sonya . . . Well that she . . .?'

'Is made pregnant?' The Seducer helped him out of the embarrassment. 'We have regulated her like watchmakers. I promise you that the twenty-four hours between midnight tonight and midnight tomorrow will be the most fertile hours her body has ever known.'

'Satisfied, daddy?' Sonya said.

Boysie began to feel extreme trepidation.

'And they want *me* to be the father,' Boysie whispered to Mostyn.

It was now gone ten in the evening. Following their return from the capsule, the party decided that Boysie should have at least a minimum of training. Watched by the Seducer, Sorcerer, and later, the Silversmith and Solomon, Boysie tumbled around in a weightless condition inside a simulator.

'You have to give them credit,' he said, later, to Mostyn. 'They've got every mod. con.'

'You launch tomorrow afternoon at two o'clock?' said Mostyn.

'On board at noon, into the stratosphere at two. That's the plan.'

'I don't really see you as an astronaut, lad. Not you at all, so I'd better call down the strike at thirteen hundred hours tomorrow. One o'clock. Does that suit?'

'It suits fine, but for heaven's sake get it right,' said Boysie. 'If you happen to slip up I'm going to have a harrowing experience, apart from the possible paternity suit and that's a thing I've always managed to avoid.'

'Bully for you.' Mostyn's face assumed the attitude of one whose nose has been offended. 'I can send a signal at midnight tonight.'

'Well, you're not sending it from here. If they've got any little antennae around you might just get caught, and we wouldn't want you getting picked up here would we?'

'It's bloody cold out there.'

'It'll be bloody cold in the grave, cocker.'

It took a considerable time to get Mostyn to quit his room, and finally when Boysie did manage to help him out of the window it was with a certain amount of concern.

Mostyn had a happy knack of making one feel guilty even when you were in the right.

'Don't blame me if I get picked up by those dogs before I send for assistance,' Mostyn said swinging one leg over the sill into the freezing night air.

'Well that'll be two of us up the creek,' hissed Boysie.

Once Mostyn had gone, Boysie began to get the jitters. Mostyn could be a perverse blighter. Perhaps he would not even call in the NATO troops. Perhaps this was just the kind of situation in which he might revel. Watching Boysie being blasted into space never to return.

The possibility etched its way through Boysie's dreams during the shallow sleep of night.

Mostyn was not as perverse as Boysie imagined. After

slinking away from the Headquarters Building, skulking upwind from the dogs, Mostyn made his way to a point which gave him a good view of the launch site. The whole area was floodlit, and, from his position, in a slight rise about three hundred yards from Launch Control, he could see the technicians still at work on the gantry.

Mostyn wrapped himself in the sleeping bag, which had been provided at Spitzbergen, and waited patiently for midnight, the witching hour when he could make contact.

Midnight came and Mostyn began to transmit. Ten minutes later he settled down in an attempt to sleep, happy that at one o'clock on the following day three hundred airborne troops would fall from the skies. Then there would be a reckoning for people like Gravestone, Schneider, Humperdinck and Solomon.

Mostyn dozed.

Boysie finally fell into a deep sleep, dreamless and un-troubled. The sleep set in around four in the morning, and when his arm was roughly shaken he had the feeling of having shut his eyes for a moment.

'For heaven's sake I've just got to sleep.' He grumbled at the hand that bounced him back and forward on the pillow.

'Come on, Oakes. Time to go,' said Solomon abrasively.

'What? What time?' Boysie squinted at his wrist watch as memory began to slide back into his mind.

'It's only nine-thirty,' he said, a twinge of fear contract-ing his stomach. 'Don't get on board until noon.'

'Plans are changed, comrade.' Solomon was grinning. 'The count down got ahead of itself. A couple of hours ahead. Sonya is getting ready now. I've got your suit here.'

Boysie sat bolt upright, the small hairs on the back of his neck tingling as the full implications of the situation caught hold. The count down advanced by two hours.

That would mean lift off around noon. A good hour before Mostyn had ordered the strike.

'Bloody hell,' Boysie murmured. Nausea filtering physically into his throat. 'Great steaming hell.'

'Out of it,' commanded Solomon.

Boysie looked up at him. 'It's all right for you . . .' he started.

Far away above the launch site Mostyn peered down at the suddenly renewed activity which seemed to surround the cold finger of the launch vehicle.

CHAPTER TEN

SKY-CHILD

As though the sky could raise
And pluck the child from earth . . .
REPORT ON THE SOLAR SYSTEM: Joseph Jennings

BOYSIE looked in wonder, at the silver pressure suit and white visored helmet which Solomon had placed on the bed.

'I said, out of it,' repeated Solomon.

Boysie began to hedge for time. He propped himself on one elbow and peered from the bed on to the floor immediately below. Standing by the bed were a pair of weighted silver boots, essential for the well-dressed astronaut. Trouble in trumps this meant. Trouble neoned large. Trouble wall to wall.

'Do I have to pull you out?' Solomon advanced.

'Pull? No. No, not at all. You think I'm . . .'

'Chicken? Yes,' replied Solomon.

Boysie pretended that he had not heard. Like an ostrich he decided that the problem would go away if he did not acknowledge it. He slid his legs over the side of the bed. The floor beneath felt wonderfully stable in comparison to the space capsule which waited to receive him. Like a motorist heading for an inescapable collision he still told himself that this could not be happening to him.

'I've got time to shave?' he asked.

'You've time to shave and read this.' Solomon held out a slim folder.

Boysie stretched out his hand. Inside the folder was one sheet of foolscap, heavily typed.

The dossier on Sonya's sexual responses.

'Christ,' said Boysie. 'What's this? *Colour response*: light-blue.'

Solomon indicated the chair. It was festooned with a nylon vest and male briefs both in fetching duck egg blue. Boysie continued to read. 'Hey,' he commented, '*High response to the scent of leather*.'

Solomon held up a small bottle.

'After shave. Smells like leather. Use it,' he said. Then as though suddenly remembering, he took out a tiny pillbox and handed it to Boysie.

'What's this?' Boysie unscrewed the cap. Two small tablets nestled on cotton wool.

'Just take them,' said Solomon.

'For what?'

'For you. Make you horny.'

'Don't bloody need it.' Boysie was reading on. The dossier laid bare some surprising revelations. Sonya could, for instance, be taken to a high degree of sexual awareness by rubbing the inside of her right elbow or stroking the inside of her left forearm.

'You learn something new every day, don't you?' Boysie grinned. He was really taking his time.

'Five minutes to shave. That's all I give you.' Solomon sounded like a warder in the condemned cell. Which, under the circumstances, he might well be.

Boysie nervously washed, shaved, applied the leathery aftershave and fiddled about generally milking the business dry. But Solomon was breathing down his neck.

'Get into those poufy drawers and the space clobber. And hurry.'

Boysie pulled on the nylon briefs, and slipped into the silver coverall, hung about with leads and jacks which would eventually provide him with heat and oxygen during the first part of the trip. He drew up the zipper, sat down on the bed and reached for the left boot. Misjudging the weight, the boot fell from his shaking fingers.

'What the hell you put in this? Grapeshot?' Boysie looked hurt and tried again. This time, success.

When both the boots were on, Solomon began chivvying again.

'Pick up the helmet and let's get this show on the road.'

Boysie stood up. He had taken just about enough from the sinister Solomon. Confirmed coward as he was, Boysie still reacted to certain situations with blind, pigheaded violence, as a small boy is goaded into lashing out furiously and irrationally at a playground enemy.

'Look,' started Boysie. 'What gives with you, Solomon? You treat me like somebody turned over a stone and found me.'

'Didn't they?' A twisted sneer on his face.

Boysie stepped forward, cross, angry, and scared stiff. A combination of emotions which could lead either to complete violence or a nervous jibbering breakdown. Solomon's hand darted towards his pocket. An ugly Luger automatic appeared in his hand, the muzzle only inches from Boysie's tense stomach.

'Just hold it there, Oakes. Let's keep the party clean, hu?'

The Luger did it. In the flash of truth which came immediately before action, Boysie heard the voices of countless instructors. *A man with a gun feels that he is in command. He has the advantage and time is working for him. He is concentrating on his weapon, banking on it to do the work for him. The best time to make a move is while your assailant is talking. He will still take action, react. But he will have to switch his thoughts from what he is saying to what he must do about your move. This takes time. A fraction of a second maybe. But in that tiny segment of time you have a minute advantage.*

'Move quickly, Oakes.' Solomon was still talking.

Boysie heard the instructions on the psychology of weaponless defence rip through his mind, faster than light.

Automatically, he moved. A quick step to the left, at the same time pivoting to the right, stepping outside Solomon's gun hand and bringing his left hand down hard on the man's right wrist, thumb over the back, fingers round Solomon's wrist.

Boysie continued to pivot, swinging on the right foot. Both hands were now on Solomon's gun hand, pulling at his arm, and causing him to stumble.

Stepping back with his left foot, Boysie again pulled hard on the gun hand, twisting it down, then up so that all balance went.

Solomon let out a cry as the Luger was wrenched from his grasp. Boysie now only saw a mist of red anger. Solomon falling forward on his knees. The feel of cold metal in Boysie's hand. Boysie raised the gun and felt the impact, through his fingers and wrist, as he brought the weapon down with force on the back of his assailant's neck.

Solomon grunted but did not go down completely. Boysie raised the gun again, but Solomon had already taken action, his hands and arms wrapping around Boysie's legs.

Now Boysie was off balance, falling backwards. In the split second, he twisted to the right, hand raised. A second thud as the gun barrel made contact with the side of Solomon's head. Again a grunt and this time Solomon fell. Boysie, balance recovered, lifted the gun again, and again. There was blood on the side of Solomon's face. A third time, Boysie lashed out. Solomon rolled over and stayed very still. Boysie swallowed and struggled for breath.

Panic now seized him. Out. He had to get out. Out, out and away. He looked down at the smitten Solomon.

Then at the gun. A moment of indecision finally crystallizing into the same old message. Get out. Get out now.

Boysie stowed the pistol into his zip pocket on the left thigh of the pressurized suit, plucked up his helmet and slipped quietly from the room. His plans were vague and undecided and he began to make his way up the passage with a certain unnatural stealth. Coming to the turning which led on to the main corridor, and so to the foyer, Boysie decided to bluff his way out.

Taking a lungful of air he began to walk purposefully to the main entrance foyer. A few yards from the doors he could see that one of the ubiquitous Landrovers was waiting outside, its driver stamping up and down in the cold.

Boysie passed through the doors and approached the Landrover.

'Solomon says we've got to carry on,' he lied, blank faced, to the driver.

'Wish he'd make up his mind.' The driver looked ill tempered. 'That's three times the orders've been changed today.' He spoke with a slight accent which could have been French.

'And where do you come from?' Boysie asked, trying to sound interested as he took his seat in the vehicle.

'Avignon,' answered the terse driver.

'Dancing bridge country, eh?'

The driver spat, put the Landrover into gear and set off with a screeching of tyres. Boysie waited until they were clear of the headquarters complex, on to the dirt road. His move had to be made when out of sight from both the HQ Building and the Launch site. Slowly his hand moved towards the thigh pocket. He shifted in his seat as the hand quickly unzipped the pocket.

'Let's pull up here, shall we?' Boysie said pleasantly, pushing the gun into the driver's ribs. The man looked down, verified that it was a real firearm which threatened his kidneys, and braked, hurriedly, to a standstill.

'What's the idea?'

'The idea, old Avignon mate, is to stop me taking a leap into space with a bleeding great rocket up my arse.'

The driver spat again.

'I think we'll take a little walk, eh? Over there where we can lie up until it's all too late.'

The driver shrugged and climbed down, Boysie never letting the pistol stray from his back. Moving forward, they faced each other in front of the bonnet.

'Come on then. Walk,' instructed Boysie.

The driver smirked and looked past Boysie's left shoulder. 'It's too old a trick, chum. Let's get moving.'

'It is also an old mistake.' The voice came from behind and at the same moment a hard metallic piece of equipment tickled Boysie's spine.

'Drop the gun,' said the voice. Boysie dropped the Luger.

'Now you can turn round.'

Boysie turned. One of the parka-clad gents with the white identity circles faced him. The driver moved in front, now carrying Boysie's discarded Luger.

'Okay,' said Boysie. 'As they say in the best gangster movies, it's a fair cop.'

'Into the truck,' said the guard.

'Get in,' repeated the driver.

Boysie complied, the guard climbing up behind him.

'All roadways are under constant surveillance,' said the guard as they took off up the track. 'Silly of you to try anything.'

Boysie remained silent. He could but agree.

The driver, with Solomon's gun, held Boysie in his seat when they arrived at the complex. The guard disappeared, returning with the Silversmith.

Sir Bruce looked livid.

'What the hell're you playing at?' He reached up and was about to yank Boysie from his seat when the Sorcerer appeared behind him.

'Silversmith. No, you might ruin a good pressure suit.'

'Christ,' murmured Boysie. 'It's the pressure suit they're worrying about, not me.'

'Why have you done this?' asked the Sorcerer.

'To hell with him,' the Silversmith ranted. 'After all the work, you have to land us with an idiot like this.'

The Sorcerer remained calm. 'I am sure he's not an idiot. Why did you do it, Apprentice? Why?'

Boysie did a quick appreciation of the situation. At the moment he was alive. By the looks of him, the foul Sir Bruce Gravestone would not rest until the situation was reversed. That would make an untidy bullet through the windpipe, or worse. The butterflies began to do press-ups and forward rolls inside his guts. On the other hand, thought Boysie, if one could manage to spin life out, then there was always the slender chance that he could do the space capsule bit and live.

'I'm sorry,' he blurted out, 'just panic. Plain ordinary panic.'

'Yellow livered bastard,' spluttered the Silversmith.

'I'm all right now,' said Boysie, his complexion belying the words.

'You think I'm going to trust you in that Capsule after this?' The Silversmith looked at him with contempt.

'I can't see that you can do anything else.' Boysie prepared to play his trump card. 'Your experts chose me. They trust me. It was only one second of panic.' Boysie took a deep breath before adding, 'Only panic, Sir Bruce.'

The Silversmith went a mild grey colour. 'What did you call me?'

'Sir Bruce Gravestone. Like this gentleman is called von Humperdinck and your Seducer is a Professor Schneider.'

'And how did you know that?'

'My job concerns astronautics and its allied sciences, Sir Bruce,' Boysie lied happily. 'It is my business to know these things.'

The Silversmith spluttered. Even the Sorcerer looked concerned. The pause was magnificently pregnant.

'Get him into the rocket. And I hope he burns.' The Silversmith turned on his heel.

'You don't mean that Sir . . . Silversmith,' shouted the Sorcerer. 'It must be a success.'

Gravestone stopped and turned. 'You're quite right.' He looked at Boysie. 'This has got to be a success. There's far too much at stake. Financially I mean. I have always been a gambler. Now I'm putting a fortune on you.' He paused again before turning and stumping his way towards the Launch Control Building.

'Come.' The Sorcerer took Boysie's arm. 'Your young woman is waiting. Make it good, eh? Make it good and there will be great rewards.'

Not even the thought of great rewards could ward off hypertension which was building up inside Boysie.

Sonya waited for them in the lift cage below the gantry. The Sorcerer patted his shoulder. Sonya gave him a timid smile. Boysie comforted himself with the thought that she must be as frightened as him. They entered the cage. The door slid forward, the clang of a tomb closing, and they began the journey upwards.

'Only an hour to launch,' said the Sorcerer, excitedly.

Boysie's stomach refused to join his body on the upward journey, it stayed resolutely on the ground. Grief, he thought, if it does that for an elevator ride what the hell's it going to do when they push me up to the heavens?

Mostyn was getting cramp in his right forearm. He rubbed it hard with his left hand, then returned to his viewing position. It was all disconcerting. Things were beginning to happen down there. It was all taking place too soon. The strike force was over an hour away, yet Boysie and the girl were already being taken up to the capsule. Mostyn bit his lip in a worried gesture and peered through the binoculars.

He did not even hear the movement behind him. The first he knew of the two guards was the prickle among the short hairs behind his neck, followed by the tingle of metal on skin.

'What have we here?' said one of the guards. He had a mild Cockney accent.

'A spy?' The other guard sounded quite cultured. A slight accent. A well-taught Swede, thought Mostyn.

'On your feet.' The first guard prodded with his rifle. Slowly, Mostyn stood up.

'What are you doing here?' The first guard again.

'Bird watching,' replied Mostyn through his teeth.

'We shall see. Walk.'

Mostyn had no choice. He walked, cursing Boysie with some violence.

It was not so much fear that coursed through Boysie's mind and body as he settled into the pilot's seat of Sext. It was more on the lines of stark terror.

Inside the helmet it seemed stifling. He glanced across at Sonya. She gave him another timid smile and put out her silver gloved hand. He felt it on his knee and placed his hand over hers, giving it what was meant to be a re-assuring pat.

A technician was bending over the cockpit, making sure that the safety harness was tight and that the heat and oxygen supply lines were plugged in.

The technician gave Boysie a final tap on the shoulder and departed.

Boysie looked down at the clip board with the neatly typed pre-launch orders. He pressed the canopy button and the reinforced perspex dome whined into place over their heads.

'Fifty minutes, ten seconds and counting,' said the controller's voice in their earphones. Less than an hour to go.

They arrived at the Launch Complex, Mostyn sweating despite the cold. One of the guards stayed with him, while the other disappeared into the Control Building.

They stood there waiting and looking at the massive gantry and its child, out on the launch pad, the long high pointing phallic symbol waiting to break the maidenhead of gravity.

The first guard returned.

'In,' he said, motioning to the Launch Control door.

The Swedish guard prodded again with his rifle.

Inside the building there was a nervous sense of tension. Passing through the small entrance hall, Mostyn was pushed forward into a large, low ceilinged room.

Dominating the scene was a long opaque projection of the world. Lights glowed red across the whole face of the map, criss-crossed with heavy white lines which seemed to emanate from a point in Southern Africa.

Directly in front of the illuminated map five men sat at a large console, in the centre a large television monitor gleamed blue. On the screen was a picture of the scene out on the launch pad.

The picture was repeated on several other smaller monitors throughout the room which was peopled by about thirty men all bent on contributing their own specialized skills and knowledge to the launch.

The Cockney guard slipped away from Mostyn, weaving between the monitors and electronics panels, towards the main control point in front of the map. He bent and whispered to one of the five controllers who stood up and followed him to the entrance where Mostyn waited at gun point. The man had got only half-way across the room before Mostyn recognized Sir Bruce Gravestone.

Sir Bruce's face was a vivid scarlet, the colour of rage tinged with the blue of blood pressure.

'Where the hell's Solomon?' he asked the Cockney guard as they came up to Mostyn. 'Where the hell is the man? He should be dealing with this.' Then, turning to Mostyn, 'Who the hell are you and what are you doing here?'

Mostyn decided to play it innocent and vaguely outraged. 'I've been bird watching, what the devil are you doing? I shall most certainly make a complaint . . .'

'Cut the ornithologist twaddle. Ornithologists don't come in uniforms carrying weapons.'

For the first time, Mostyn realized that the Swede was carrying the haversack which he had carefully hidden under snow-bound rocks six feet or so from his observation point. The haversack contained his weapons and the other equipment, including the radio transceiver.

There was a pause. A good half-minute during which Mostyn decided on his next course of action.

'All right,' he said at last. 'You'd better know. I'm a Colonel of British Intelligence attached to AFNORTH. We've been interested in your little playground for some weeks. I might as well . . .'

'You might as well what?' Sir Bruce had bad breath and his face was close to Mostyn. 'You might as well tell me that the game is up? Is that what you were going to say?'

'Something like that.'

'No chance. No chance at all.' There was a nasty glint in the baronet's eyes. 'Nothing can stop the count-down, now, and once it's started we have three men. One in Moscow, one in London and one in Washington. They'll be making telephone calls. Your people will be interested in what we are doing. So interested that they'll call off any attempt to stop us by force.'

Mostyn opened his mouth. He was about to spill the beans on Boysie. Changing his mind he clamped his teeth together and shrugged.

The launch controller's voice echoed through the loud-speaker system. 'Ten minutes, five seconds and counting.'

Boysie would be hearing the same voice. For a moment, Mostyn spared a thought for his colleague's shattered nervous system.

The door opened and another guard came in making straight for Sir Bruce.

'Well?' asked the baronet, raising his eyebrows.

'Solomon,' said the newly arrived guard.

'What about Solomon?' Sir Bruce curt.

'Looks as though Sonya's partner injured him. They just found him in the Apprentice's room. Suspected fracture of the skull.'

'Well done, Oaksie,' breathed Mostyn.

Sir Bruce swore violently. Then turned to Mostyn. 'I suppose this is your doing?'

'Could be,' Mostyn replied happily.

The launch controller spoke again. 'Eight minutes and counting.'

'I think we'll keep you under observation here,' said Sir Bruce. 'Keep your eye on him,' he looked at the Cock-ney guard, 'and bring him over to the controller's con-sole.'

The guard began prodding again. Mostyn obediently followed Sir Bruce to the launch controller's table. The controller and his assistant were nameless faces, but the other two men at the control console were recognizable as von Humperdinck and Schneider.

Sir Bruce pointed to an empty swivel chair next to his own. 'Sit there. Keep still. Keep quiet.'

Mostyn could do nothing more than obey, and hope for the arrival of the NATO strike forces.

The sonorous voice of the controller still told off the minutes and seconds as they clicked away on the digital computer on the panel in front of them. Mostyn found it hard to believe that Boysie was at the receiving end of the count-down.

'Two minutes and ten seconds ... and counting ... one minute and thirty seconds ...' The tension became unbearable, Mostyn's palms damp with sweat. 'One minute ... thirty seconds ... Fifteen seconds ... Ten ... Nine ... Eight ... Seven ... Six ... Five ... Four ... Three ... Two ... One ... Ignition ... Lift off.'

On the screen in front of them the great rocket splayed out a massive low mushroom of smoke. It trembled against the gantry. The umbilical cable dropped free and the huge metal finger began to rise, straight and true. Mostyn could not take his eyes from the screen. The rocket, still trembling, accelerated, then began to whistle away, riding on a spear of flame.

'All systems go,' said the controller, his eyes flicking along the console which registered reports from the other computers and consoles in the building. 'He's on track. Sky-Child One do you read? Do you read?'

Boysie had heard the controller count off the seconds. He could also hear his own heart. It seemed to have risen from its natural place to settle in his throat. His whole body heaved with apprehension. Then came the terrifying judder as though he was balanced on a dozen pneumatic drills. The turbulence built up with terrifying speed. Boysie could feel his teeth chattering. He glanced at Sonya who was staring straight ahead, yet she seemed to be shivering. The whole cockpit vibrated. Boysie's breathing was rapid inside the helmet. There was a sense of disintegration. Then, as suddenly as it had built up, the juddering stopped and they sat quiet with no sense of movement and no sign of power except a whine, like a large vacuum cleaner.

'All systems are go.' The voice of the controller came loud within Boysie's helmet.

'Stage two rocket . . . On.'

There was another bout of shaking. Not so long this time as the second stage rocket blew them high and into orbit over the Indian Ocean.

Then the magic words of the controller. 'Okay to leave Sext. You are clear to leave Sext.'

Boysie looked over at Sonya who nodded. Hands down to the canopy release. The canopy slid back. Sonya twisted her harness release and punched the circular retaining ring in front of her. The harness dropped away. Boysie followed suit and they both began their climb on to the aluminium ladders which ran from the capsule's neck down into the capsule itself.

It took time to negotiate the ladders. Boysie moved slowly, one foot following the other in a careful precision, in order to remain balanced. He could feel the magnetic weights clamping against metal as he reached the bottom of the ladder, yet the whole feeling was as though he were attempting to walk under water. The surrounding atmosphere seemed to be constantly lifting him so that only the boots remained anchored. His body wavered like a water weed floating back and forth with a changeable eddy.

Boysie stood like this for a moment at the foot of the ladder. Trying to remember the sequence of events through which he now had to move. Hand up to the bulkhead closing lever. Pull down. Noiselessly the heavy metal panels closed off the capsule's neck. Above him the sign flashed on. PRESSURE SUITS AND HELMETS CAN BE REMOVED. BEWARE WEIGHTLESS CONDITION.

Carefully, Boysie clanked his way towards the big leather couch. Sonya was already there removing her helmet. Boysie followed suit, sitting on the edge of the couch. Above them the control panel was lit up. Next to a sign reading ORBIT NUMBER was the figure one.

'You all right?' asked Boysie amazed that his voice sounded so steady.

'I'm fine. Easier than we thought.' Sonya was tossing and fluffing her hair which had a tendency to move upwards. She put out her silver gloved hand. 'Did they give you any pills?'

'Pills? Yes.' said Boysie vaguely embarrassed, remembering Solomon's explanation for the pills.

'Me, too,' smiled Sonya. 'They work don't they?'

Boysie was silent for a moment, considering. He did not really feel any different. He was his usual randy self, and danger and fear, he knew from past experience, always made him worse. As though the danger could be obscured by an attempt to return into the warm anonymity of the womb.

Well, he thought, if he had to go there was no better way. At least they would be founder members of a new society.

'Better get started then.' His voice held no trace of lechery. It was as though he was treating the whole business as a clinical exercise.

Sonya nodded and pulled down the zip on her silver pressure suit. Then she removed her gloves. Under the suit she was naked to the waist, her breasts ripe and wonderful. Boysie's eyes travelled down. She wore a thin pair of bikini briefs, jet black and trimmed with a quarter inch of lace. The picture was utterly feminine, and Boysie felt the hard natural surge of desire.

He pulled off his gloves and ripped down on the zip. Sonya reacted well to the sight of Boysie naked except for the blue briefs.

Boysie was now fumbling with his boots. First one came off, then, with a wrench, he pulled himself free of the other. Immediately he began to rise. He clutched out at the couch, missed and floated up to the roof.

'Help me, for crying out loud,' he yelled.

But Sonya was engrossed in removing her boots while still keeping a tight hold on the couch. At last her boots were off and she was clinging to the leather to stop rising.

Boysie turned his body, manoeuvring himself into a position where he could place his feet on the metal sides. Once there he settled himself into a frog-like stance and pushed off hard with his feet. Boysie's body arched down towards the couch. He lashed out with his arms trying to grab at anything solid.

His right hand made contact with Sonya's coverall, from which she was attempting to free herself. The coverall came away in his hand and he was floating upwards once more, this time carrying the pressure suit and leaving Sonya, hanging on to the couch, dressed only in her briefs and with legs rising out of control.

'This is ridiculous,' mouthed Boysie.

'Hang on. I'll try and get hold of the retaining locks for my hands and feet.' Sonya kicked, pulled and struggled her way along the side of the couch while Boysie resumed the frog position once more.

This time he made it to the couch, hanging on to one of the clamps which had been strategically placed in order to anchor Sonya in a spreadeagled position.

He pulled down and began to control his body, swinging round, opening the locker at the head of the couch and stuffing Sonya's pressure suit into the compartment provided for it. On his side of the locker was the thick pouched belt of body weights. Boysie pulled at them. The weight kept him down and after five minutes struggle he had the pressure suit off and stowed in the locker while the body weights were firmly belted round his waist.

Boysie remained still, breathing heavily after the incredible exertion. Sonya, after several attempts, was now firmly affixed to the couch.

Boysie swallowed. 'It doesn't seem fair,' he said.

'What doesn't seem fair?'

'This.' Boysie felt definitely guilty, poised above the outstretched girl. She looked incredibly desirable.

'Why doesn't it seem fair?' she asked.

'Well, it's like raping you or something. After all you're a kind of captive audience aren't you?'

'Captive, but ready to enjoy.' Her voice had taken on that smouldering quality which he had noticed during the briefing. 'I can promise you that I won't think of it as rape. We're making history.'

'A funny way. I wonder what they'll title the chapter. Space Sex?'

'Shouldn't be surprised. Come on though, Boysie. Let's do it.'

Boysie pulled down on the weighted net which hung above the couch locker. It dropped square over Sonya. And Boysie spent the next ten minutes attempting to squeeze under it. The while business seemed unreal and strange but at last he was under the weighted net, beside her on the couch.

'There must be an easier way to make money,' he said, realizing that neither of them was yet naked. Boysie turned and noted that the ORBIT NUMBER sign had now moved to two.

'Coming into second orbit.' The controller's voice rasped round the Launch Control block house.

Mostyn gazed, impressed, at the illuminated map which was tracing the capsule's course.

'How can you track it?' He sounded almost friendly asking Sir Bruce.

'Ah. You see what you're up against now do you? We have eighteen tracking stations set along the orbit. South

America, Africa, India, Malaysia, New Guinea. It is all calculated to the fraction.'

A telephone shrilled near Sir Bruce's elbow. He picked it up. 'Yes? Good. All three. Good.' Replacing the receiver, Sir Bruce turned to Mostyn. 'Our operatives in Moscow, America and Britain have reported. The capsule and its contents is now under auction. In the Kremlin, the Pentagon and the Ministry of Defence they'll be digging out their pockets.' He laughed.

'I don't think they'll dig too deeply.' Mostyn sounded flat, as though he did not believe what he was saying.

A second later and the situation was suddenly reversed, and he knew the end was in sight.

The telephone rang out again. Gravestone lifted it and Mostyn could hear agitated noises coming from the receiver.

'Damn.' Sir Bruce looked up sharply at Mostyn, then he turned to von Humperdinck and Schneider. 'The northern look-out reports a force of three C-119Fs and three C-47s heading low towards us. Can we re-position the capsule?'

Schneider's face went white. 'They can't. No one can stop this now. No one. I will *not* allow it.'

'It's not for us to allow.' Ellerman von Humperdinck whirled his chair around. For a second, Mostyn could not believe what he saw, a neat silver Browning cupped in von Humperdinck's hand. He stepped back, moving into a corner. The whole room had gone silent but for the whisper of heaters.

The guard behind Mostyn moved, Mostyn sensing that he was taking a quick aim on Humperdinck, threw himself back, his head catching the man's stomach. There was the whump of two explosions in the confined space. The guard's bullet went wild but Humperdinck's hit its mark. The guard was lifted backwards to drop into an untidy heap behind the main console.

'His rifle, Colonel Mostyn,' rapped von Humperdinck.

Mostyn grabbed the rifle and turned, backing towards Humperdinck.

'All of you,' said Mostyn. 'All of you get your hands in the air.'

'One moment,' von Humperdinck chimed in. 'All of you except the launch controller. We need him to get the capsule and Sext down in one piece.'

But the controller was a jump ahead. His hands snaked out to the controls on the console. A high-pitched whine began to rise into a crescendo and the instruments on the console appeared to be going wild. At the same moment there was an explosion from outside the blockhouse.

'Sounds like the 5th Cavalry have arrived in the nick of time,' muttered Mostyn.

'Too late for our friends in the capsule,' Humperdinck was shouting. 'Stand still everybody.'

Schneider, taking the opportunity afforded by the controller's sudden movement leaped forward towards Mostyn. Mostyn's bullet caught Schneider in the throat, his gurgle lasting as a reflex for a good half-minute after life had left him.

'Now don't let anyone else try it,' said Mostyn. 'A NATO force will have landed by now. They are under orders to take as many prisoners as possible. And you,' he nodded towards Sir Bruce, 'are all mine, baby.'

Sir Bruce gave a snort of defeat.

'What about the capsule?' Mostyn asked Humperdinck out of the corner of his mouth.

'It depends. By now they will have received a signal telling them that ground control has been abandoned. If they are sensible enough they can set the re-entry system manually, but where they'll land is anybody's guess.'

'And what of you?' asked Mostyn. 'How come you changed sides?'

'I will accept the jail sentence which will undoubtedly

come my way. I ceased to be in sympathy with these people when Miss Challis died.'

Mostyn nodded and leaned back against the wall, his rifle muzzle swinging in a lazy arc, covering the remaining staff of the launch control blockhouse. Soon the NATO force would push their way in, but the unnatural warble still continued from the controller's console.

Two pairs of briefs, one blue and one black, floated, almost waltzed, in the air above the leather couch. Boysie watched them, fascinated. His concentration broken by a low warble which gradually built up inside the capsule. Not at first understanding, Boysie's gaze fell upon the control panel. The ORBIT NUMBER sign still read two. Then, as the warble became more intense, a red sign started to flash on and off. GROUND CONTROL CEASED the sign read.

'Christ,' said Boysie, a definite shake in his voice. 'What does that mean?'

Sonya shifted uncomfortably. 'Something's gone wrong at the launch control. It means we're on our own.'

'Oh, no.' Boysie felt he had lived it all before, but this time the business was lifted to nightmare proportions. They were alone, cut off from control. 'What do we do?' he asked, lost.

'I suppose we activate the re-entry system by hand. The control is up there. It gives us ninety minutes to establish ourselves in Sext. Once Sext is clear I suppose you fly and let down at the first airfield we come on.'

'I had an idea this might happen,' said Boysie. 'And I've got news for you. I can't fly.'

'That's great,' said Sonya. 'That I really like. Well, you'll have to try won't you?'

Boysie nodded and reached out for the re-entry control system. Humperdinck had gone through the drill many times and it was second nature for Boysie to turn the system on.

Now they began the long, difficult, and involved process of dressing themselves in a weightless atmosphere.

They managed to drag on their coveralls and get back into their weighted boots after a half-hour's struggle. Ten minutes later, in helmets, they began the climb back into Sext, neat and snug in the neck of the capsule.

After one hour they had managed to harness themselves into the cockpit. One hour ten minutes saw them closing the canopy once more.

Boysie struggled to remember the order of actions to be carried out within Sext before the re-entry phase.

Rocket motor throttle fully opened, turbojet throttles half open. Gear up and locked. All they could do now was to wait. Soon their great push would come and they would be truly on their own.

Mostyn stood with the commander of the AFNORTH force. Below, on the beach, troops had begun to escort their prisoners to the waiting boats which in turn, would ferry them to the four destroyers which lay at anchor off Wizard.

'That's all we can do,' said the commander, a gaunt, pock-marked Brigadier. 'I've ordered all NATO commands to pass the message to all airfields, radar stations and civil airlines. They will be prepared for a fast, semi-controlled lifting body. I only wish we could pin-point the re-entry area.'

'Perhaps one of the observatories will lock on to them,' Mostyn knew he was being optimistic.

'They might,' replied the Brigadier. 'They just might.'

Deep down, Mostyn knew that there was little hope, even if somebody locked on to the craft. Boysie could not possibly get the thing down in one piece.

It was like being thumped in the small of the back by a giant wielding a massive plank. The sensation winded Boysie. They seemed to be thrown about inside the cockpit of Sext. Then from the subdued light inside the capsule's neck, they were shot out into the atmosphere, into clear bright light which almost burned through the protective visors of their helmets.

Boysie thought for a second, that this must be the same sensation felt by a circus human cannonball. They had a sense of speed, as though they were ripping the air, rending it apart.

Then, the roar of the rocket motor died, to be replaced by the steady drumming of the turbojets.

Boysie's hands fell on to the control yoke and his feet nestled on to the rudder pedals.

Easing back the yoke Boysie found that the craft's nose lifted. He gently tested the yaw that could be produced by moving the rudder pedestal which divided his side of the cockpit from Sonya. Easing back on the throttles he found he could reduce the engine speed.

For ten minutes, Boysie concentrated on the controls, keeping the aircraft in a shallow dive and watching the long vertical altimeter which showed they were still flying at the impossible height of 300,000 feet, or fifty miles high. Below lay an immensely beautiful sight, clear fine atmosphere right down to the curve of the earth overhung by clouds.

'Wish to hell I knew where to point this thing,' said Boysie.

'Don't worry about which way to point her, just keep her level.' Sonya sounded quite calm.

Boysie was, in fact, surprised that he was not disturbed. The immensity of the situation reduced any terror to an absurdity. Perhaps, he thought, this is the real moment of truth. The moment when one is faced by the majesty of creation beside which a human was as a tiny expendable ant.

Sext continued its slow descent. As they got lower, so they began to feel the speed. Fifty thousand feet slid past. Twenty-five thousand and they were dropping fast into cloud.

Jodrell Bank picked up the craft before anyone else. If it proceeded on its present trajectory, they warned, it would be dangerously low on the outskirts of London.

BOAC Super VC10 flight Alpha Lima, inbound from New York, was nosing into the cloud at the first stage of her let-down over the Irish Sea. Captain Hennesy and his first officer were carrying out their routine procedure with care.

Then the blip suddenly appeared on the radar scope. Large, fast and travelling from behind them on exactly the same course.

Captain Hennesy was a steady man who in many thousands of flying hours, had never experienced anything like this. He dipped the VC10's nose sharply, steepening his angle of descent. With an ear-splitting whoosh the thing passed over them. A silver comet flying on a lance of flame.

'Kee-rist,' ejaculated Captain Hennesy. 'It's the end of the world.'

The VC10 flight Alpha Lima reported immediately to London Radar Controller. Almost at the same moment the blip came up on the radar scopes in the normally quiet unpanicable Heathrow Control Tower.

'Green fields,' shouted Boysie. 'Could be England.' He was getting a lot of static in his earphones now. They dropped lower and lower and he could make out roads, rivers, woods, the whole panoply of colour.

'Shout if you see an airfield.' He looked towards Sonya who nodded.

Throttling back, Boysie scanned the closing horizon for some open space. Instead of space there was a vast growing area of houses. Houses and roads everywhere he looked and they were getting nearer all the time.

The London Radar Director flashed a diversion warning to all aircraft in the holding patterns. Calmly the Boeings and VC10s were being shuttled out of the way.

In Sext, Boysie narrowed his eyes. The roof tops were coming up fast.

'Christ,' he shouted. 'That's the bloody House of Commons ahead. We're going to clobber Big Ben. Hope they're sitting, we can get rid of this bloody government once and for all.'

He lifted Sext's nose and opened the throttles slightly, sensing, as he did so, that he was beginning to lose power. Big Ben, he thought. If that's Big Ben then Heathrow can't be far behind.

Almost as he thought it, Boysie saw the flat area, the buildings and the two long runways of twenty-eight left and twenty-eight right, which was London Airport.

Suddenly the throbbing of engines tailed off. Boysie lifted the nose and felt the machine sink under him. They were at about two thousand feet now and a good mile from the edge of twenty-eight left at which Boysie was aiming the craft's nose.

Sext sank slowly and out of control. At the last minute, Boysie made a final attempt. He put down the undercarriage and prayed as never before.

A row of red slated roofs came up to his left. He was almost level with them. People were running on the road below. Cars and buses. Hideously close. Then, as if by a miracle, the threshold slid past and Boysie was looking at the wonderful sight of an empty, almost eternal runway ahead.

He closed the throttles, held the control yoke steady and felt the strange craft gently transfer its weight from the little stub wings to the undercarriage.

They were still moving and the runway would almost certainly run out before they came to a standstill, but Boysie was unconcerned.

It was only later, after they had climbed from the cabin, and dropped from Sext, now nose down in a ditch two hundred yards from the end of the runway, that Boysie began to react. His hands and legs shook as they had never shaken before.

An ambulance drew up. They found the girl, Sonya, at ease and co-operative. But the pilot was coughing his heart up between bouts of nervous vomiting.

The ambulance man thought he heard the pilot muttering obscenities connected with the name Mostyn.

CHAPTER ELEVEN

SEQUEL

'It seems,' said Mostyn, 'that in the eyes of the Pentagon you are a hero.'

'Don't see what all the fuss is about,' Boysie cast his eyes down modestly.

They were gathered, Mostyn, Boysie, Griffin and Chicory – the last two having finally made it back to London – in Mostyn's favourite restaurant, an Italian eating house hard by Marble Arch.

It was early evening. During the day, Mostyn and Boysie had both been summoned to give evidence against Sir Bruce Gravestone whose sentence for high treason, together with four cronies, looked like being a stiff one.

The following week, Boysie and Mostyn were again scheduled to give evidence. This time before a Grand Jury in Washington where Ellerman von Humperdinck was to be arraigned on similar charges.

'Personally, I do not see what the fuss is about, either,' said Mostyn. 'But they want you to receive, with the lovely Sonya, some insignia which will mark you both as founder members of the *Hundred Miles Up Club*.'

'So that yer'll both be in the club,' mused Griffin with a revolting leer.

'Is she . . .?' began Chicory looking open mouthed at Boysie, anger spreading on her face.

'No,' said Boysie quietly. 'No, she isn't. To tell you the truth, the old Sorcerer, Seducer and Silversmith mucked things up. What with the weightlessness and all, it's not really possible.'

'What a shame,' smiled Mostyn. 'Do you mean that we're not going to be blessed with Son of Boysie Oakes?'

'Neither son nor daughter.' Boysie turned towards Chicory. 'We have some unfinished business, I believe.'

The waiters hovered like vultures.

'Your treat, I think.' Boysie grinned at Mostyn and took Chicory by the arm.

'One day,' said Mostyn grimly, 'one day, Oakes, I'll have you. On toast I'll have you.'

A SELECTION OF FINE READING
AVAILABLE IN CORGI BOOKS

Novels

☐ 552 07763 1	ANOTHER COUNTRY	*James Baldwin* 5/-
☐ 552 07938 3	THE NAKED LUNCH	*William Burroughs* 7/6
☐ 552 07317 2	THE CHINESE ROOM	*Vivian Connell* 5/-
☐ 552 08296 1	THE ROUND TOWER	*Catherine Cookson* 6/-
☐ 552 08108 6	HOLD MY HAND I'M DYING	*John Gordon Davis* 7/6
☐ 552 07777 1	THE WAR BABIES	*Gwen Davis* 5/-
☐ 552 08183 3	BOYS AND GIRLS TOGETHER	*William Goldman* 7/6
☐ 552 07968 5	THE WELL OF LONELINESS	*Radclyffe Hall* 7/6
☐ 552 08125 6	CATCH 22	*Joseph Heller* 7/-
☐ 552 07913 5	MOTHERS AND DAUGHTERS	*Evan Hunter* 7/6
☐ 552 08252 X	HESTER ROON	*Norah Lofts* 6/-
☐ 552 08291 0	MADSELIN	*Norah Lofts* 5/-
☐ 552 08002 0	MY SISTER, MY BRIDE	*Edwina Marks* 5/-
☐ 552 08253 8	THE BREAKING STRAIN	*John Masters* 5/-
☐ 552 08164 7	ALL SAUCE FOR THE GANDER	*Nan Maynard* 5/-
☐ 552 08092 6	THINKING GIRL	*Norma Meacock* 5/-
☐ 552 07594 9	HAWAII (colour illustrations)	*James A. Michener* 10/6
☐ 552 08124 8	LOLITA	*Vladimir Nabokov* 6/-
☐ 552 08218 X	WHEN FLAMINGOS FALL	*Mark Oliver* 5/-
☐ 552 08311 9	WITH MY BODY	*David Pinner* 5/-
☐ 552 08310 0	RAMAGE AND THE DRUMBEAT	*Dudley Pope* 5/-
☐ 552 07954 5	RUN FOR THE TREES	*James Rand* 7/6
☐ 552 08289 9	GOODBYE, COLUMBUS	*Philip Roth* 5/-
☐ 552 07655 4	THE HONEY BADGER	*Robert Ruark* 7/6
☐ 552 08231 7	THE DAUGHTERS OF LONGING	*Froma Sand* 6/-
☐ 552 08298 8	SUCH AS WE	*Pierre Sichel* 7/-
☐ 552 08324 0	ONE FOR SORROW	*Joyce Stranger* 4/-
☐ 552 08325 9	THE WAYWARD BUS	*John Steinbeck* 5/-
☐ 552 07807 7	VALLEY OF THE DOLLS	*Jacqueline Susann* 7/6
☐ 552 08013 6	THE EXHIBITIONIST	*Henry Sutton* 7/6
☐ 552 08217 1	THE CARETAKERS	*Dariel Telfer* 7/-
☐ 552 08091 8	TOPAZ	*Leon Uris* 7/6
☐ 552 08073 X	THE PRACTICE	*Stanley Winchester* 7/6
☐ 552 07116 1	FOREVER AMBER Vol. 1	*Kathleen Winsor* 5/-
☐ 552 07117 X	FOREVER AMBER Vol. II	*Kathleen Winsor* 5/-
☐ 552 07790 9	THE BEFORE MIDNIGHT SCHOLAR	*Li Yu* 7/6

War

☐ 552 08190 6	THE ADMIRAL	*Martin Dibner* 7/–
☐ 552 08315 1	THE SAVAGES	*Ronald Hardy* 6/–
☐ 552 08168 X	MONTE CASSINO	*Sven Hassel* 5/–
☐ 552 08159 0	THE WILLING FLESH	*Willi Heinrich* 6/–
☐ 552 08222 8	SAGITTARIUS RISING	*Cecil Lewis* 5/–
☐ 552 08299 6	THE BRIDGES AT TOKO RI	*James A. Michener* 4/–
☐ 552 08221 X	GIMME THE BOATS	*J. E. Macdonnell* 5/–
☐ 552 07726 7	THE DIRTY DOZEN	*E. M. Nathanson* 7/6
☐ 552 08255 4	THE ENEMY SKY	*Peter Saxon* 4/–
☐ 552 08314 3	JOURNEY'S END	*R. C. Sherriff & Vernon Bartlett* 5/–
☐ 552 08169 8	633 SQUADRON	*Frederick E. Smith* 5/–
☐ 552 08078 0	TREBLINKA (illustrated)	*Jean Francois Steiner* 7/6
☐ 552 08113 2	THE LONG NIGHT'S WALK	*Alan White* 4/–

Romance

☐ 552 08264 3	HIGHLAND INTERLUDE	*Lucilla Andrews* 4/–
☐ 552 07434 9	WEB OF DAYS	*Edna Lee* 4/–
☐ 552 08244 9	THE TEAM	*Hilary Neal* 3/6

Science Fiction

☐ 552 08306 2	THE OTHER SIDE OF THE SKY	*Arthur C. Clarke* 4/–
☐ 552 08276 7	DANDELION WINE	*Ray Bradbury* 4/–
☐ 552 08265 1	NEW WRITINGS IN S.F.15	*Edited by John Carnell* 4/–
☐ 552 08321 6	SIX GATES FROM LIMBO	*J. T. McIntosh* 4/–
☐ 552 07682 1	THE SHAPE OF THINGS TO COME	*H. G. Wells* 7/6

General

☐ 552 07566 3	SEXUAL LIFE IN ENGLAND	*Dr. Ivan Bloch* 9/6
☐ 552 08086 1	ENQUIRE WITHIN UPON EVERYTHING	*Reference* 7/6
☐ 552 07593 0	UNMARRIED LOVE	*Dr. Eustace Chesser* 5/–
☐ 552 07950 2	SEXUAL BEHAVIOUR	*Dr. Eustace Chesser* 5/–
☐ 552 97996 1	THE ISLAND RACE (illustrated in colour)	*Winston S. Churchill* 30/–
☐ 552 96000 4	BARBARELLA (illustrated)	*Jean Claude Forest* 30/–
☐ 552 07804 2	THE BIRTH CONTROLLERS	*Peter Fryer* 7/6
☐ 552 07400 4	MY LIFE AND LOVES	*Frank Harris* 12/6
☐ 552 98121 4	FIVE GIRLS (illustrated)	*Sam Haskins* 21/–
☐ 552 97745 4	COWBOY KATE (illustrated)	*Sam Haskins* 21/–
☐ 552 98307 1	NOVEMBER GIRL (illustrated)	*Sam Haskins* 21/–
☐ 552 01541 4	MAN AND SEX	*Kaufman and Borgeson* 5/–
☐ 552 07916 2	SEXUAL RESPONSE IN WOMEN	*Drs. E. and P. Kronhausen* 9/6
☐ 552 98247 4	THE HISTORY OF THE NUDE IN PHOTOGRAPHY (illustrated)	*Peter Lacey and Anthony La Rotonda* 25/–
☐ 552 08120 5	ONE IN TWENTY	*Bryan Magee* 5/–
☐ 552 08069 1	THE OTHER VICTORIANS	*Steven Marcus* 10/–
☐ 552 08162 0	THE NAKED APE	*Desmond Morris* 6/–
☐ 552 07965 0	SOHO NIGHT AND DAY (illustrated)	*Norman and Bernard* 7/6
☐ 552 08105 1	BEYOND THE TENTH	*T. Lobsang Rampa* 5/–
☐ 552 08228 7	WOMAN; a Biological Study	*Philip Rhodes* 5/–
☐ 552 08322 4	FIFTY YEARS A MEDIUM	*Estelle Roberts* 6/–
☐ 552 98178 8	THE YELLOW STAR (illustrated)	*Gerhard Schoenberner* 21/–
☐ 552 08323 2	DOVES FOR THE SEVENTIES	*ed. Peter Robins* 5/–
☐ 552 08038 1	EROS DENIED (illustrated)	*Wayland Young* 7/6
☐ 552 07918 9	BRUCE TEGNER'S COMPLETE BOOK OF KARATE	6/–

Westerns

- 552 08082 9   **SUDDEN—APACHE FIGHTER**   *Frederick H. Christian* 4/-
- 552 08277 5   **.44 CALIBRE MAN (No. 56)**   *J. T. Edson* 4/-
- 552 08320 8   **THE RUSHERS (No. 57)**   *J. T. Edson* 4/-
- 552 08281 3   **THE FAST GUN (No. 54)**   *J. T. Edson* 4/-
- 552 08262 7   **BUTCH CASSIDY AND THE SUNDANCE KID**
  William Goldman 4/-
- 552 08270 8   **MACKENNA'S GOLD**   *Will Henry* 4/-
- 552 08302 X   **CONAGHER**   *Louis L'Amour* 4/-
- 552 08303 8   **RADIGAN**   *Louis L'Amour* 4/-
- 552 08304 6   **LANDO**   *Louis L'Amour* 4/-
- 552 08263 5   **DONOVAN'S GUN**   *Luke Short* 4/-

Crime

- 552 08272 4   **PSYCHO**   *Robert Bloch* 4/-
- 552 08301 1   **TEN DAYS TO OBLIVION**   *Michael Cooney* 4/-
- 552 08316 X   **FOUNDER MEMBER**   *John Gardner* 5/-
- 552 08004 7   **MADRIGAL**   *John Gardner* 5/-
- 552 08317 8   **THE LADY IN THE CAR WITH GLASSES AND A GUN**
  Sebastien Japrisot 4/-
- 552 08318 6   **THE 10.30 FROM MARSEILLE**   *Sebastien Japrisot* 4/-
- 552 08319 4   **TRAP FOR CINDERELLA**   *Sebastien Japrisot* 4/-
- 552 08267 8   **THE GIRL HUNTERS**   *Mickey Spillane* 4/-
- 552 08223 6   **THE DELTA FACTOR**   *Mickey Spillane* 4/-
- 552 08257 0   **THE MAN WHO KILLED HIMSELF**   *Julian Symons* 4/-

All these books are available at your bookshop or newsagent: or can be ordered direct from the publisher. Just tick the titles you want and fill in the form below.

CORGI BOOKS, Cash Sales Department, P.O. Box 11, Falmouth, Cornwall.

Please send cheque or postal order. No currency, and allow 6d. per book to cover the cost of postage and packing in U.K., 9d. per copy overseas.

NAME ....

ADDRESS ....

(DEC. '69) ....